# That Old Dead Magic
## A Rat Pack Mystery

**Books by Robert J. Randisi
(J.R. Roberts)**

*Rat Pack* mysteries

*Talbot Roper* novels

*The Gunsmith* series

*Lady Gunsmith* series

*Angel Eyes* series

*Tracker* series

*Mountain Jack Pike* series

**For more information visit:**
www.SpeakingVolumes.us

# That Old Dead Magic
## A Rat Pack Mystery

Robert J. Randisi

SPEAKING VOLUMES
NAPLES, FLORIDA
2020

That Old Dead Magic

Copyright © 2020 by Robert J. Randisi

All rights reserved. No part of this book may be
reproduced or transmitted in any form or by any means
without written permission.

ISBN 978-1-64540-225-1

To Marthayn,
the magic in my life.

*That old black magic has me in its spell,*
*That old black magic that you weave so well . . .*
Harold Arlen (music)
Johnny Mercer (lyrics)

# Prologue: August 5, 2011

*"Jerry Lewis ousted as MDA Telethon host."*

That was the headline of the story in the August 5, 2011 edition of the *L.A. Times*.

I get the Times delivered to my apartment along with several other periodicals I enjoy, including *Variety*, *Sports Illustrated*, *Playboy*, the *N.Y. Times*, the *Las Vegas Sun* and the *Las Vegas Review Journal*.

On this particular afternoon, I opened the *L.A. Times* first to have with my toast and coffee and saw the story.

At this time, Jerry was eighty-five years of age, which made us contemporaries. He had been the MDA—the Muscular Dystrophy Association—host for forty-five years, and, according to the story, they had simply dropped him. There was no statement from Jerry himself, but other show biz types—specifically other comedians—were outraged.

I've never been crazy about Jerry Lewis. But as I said, we were contemporaries, and he was one of the last remnants of the Rat Pack era alive. I had grown tired of attending funerals, and was glad he was holding on, despite several reported ailments.

Sammy had gone first in 1990, then Dino in '95 and Frank in '98. Joey hung on until 2007. (Peter Lawford had died in 1984, which I only mention because he was an early Pack member.) But Joey's funeral had been my last, and I was glad to have had the time off.

So I was hoping that something like this wouldn't cause Jerry to spiral. I mean, his performing days were probably over, so what did he have left? I had also heard that he wasn't on good terms with his sons, especially Gary. (Okay, I'm one of those people who enjoyed the music of Gary Lewis and the Playboys. Sue me). Losing the MDA relationship might be more than he could bear.

I put the *Times* down, picked up *Variety*. There was nothing in it about Jerry and the MDA parting ways, but the Vegas papers carried the story.

I took my cup and plate to the sink and rinsed them out. I had a dish washer, but didn't get much use out of it. I pretty much used the same cup, glass, plate and utensils every day.

That done, I poured myself two fingers of good bourbon and carried it back to my chair. It was my daily treat, since I didn't drink much anymore. I sipped slowly and thought . . .

I hadn't seen Jerry Lewis very much of late. I knew after he and Dean broke up their partnership and went their own ways after ten years, they didn't see each other much. What people didn't know was that they talked on the phone from time to time, but other than Frank's surprising Jerry with Dean at the '76 MDA Telethon—during which Jerry famously asked Dino, "So, ya workin'?"—and Jerry surprising Dino on stage at Bally's for his birthday in '89, they didn't see each other at all.

Jerry called Dino after his son, Dean Paul, died in that tragic plane crash, and then I saw Jerry at Dean's funeral in '95, just to nod to. I knew there was an affection between the two men that they couldn't shake, no matter how much distance was between them. And I knew that Frank and Sammy had friendships with Jerry. But I was never able to warm to him myself.

Jerry and I did spend some time together back in 1965. It was a situation I got involved in as a favor not to Dean or Jerry, but to Sammy Davis. And by the time it was over, I was even less fond of Jerry than ever . . .

# Chapter One

*Las Vegas, May 1965*

"We've got a problem," Jack Entratter said to me.

He'd sent a message down to the Sands casino floor that he needed to see me as soon as I arrived. I took the elevator to the fourth floor, waved at his girl as I entered the outer office, then went into his office when she waved me in.

Even before my butt could hit the chair, he made that announcement.

"What kind of trouble?" I asked.

"Did you see the marquee when you came in today?"

"Yes." I had wondered about it, too. It said *Sammy Davis Jr.*, and beneath that *Jerry Lewis*. "I wondered what that was about. Is Jerry part of the Summit now? And how does Dino feel about that?"

"No, Jerry's not part of the Rat Pack," Jack said. "But we needed to make some kind of change."

"Why?"

"I don't know if you noticed, but the last time the Summit was here, they didn't fill the Copa Room."

"What? How can that be?"

"It's true," Jack said. "The Rat Pack—Frank's Summit—is bringin' in less and less people." He shrugged his broad shoulders and sat back in his chair with a sour look. "People are gettin' tired of the act."

"But not of the guys," I said. "Frank and Dean, they're still as popular as ever."

"Dean more so, once his TV show premieres," Jack pointed out.

"If it's a hit."

"Oh, it will be," Jack said. "Mark my words. Unlike Frank's two series in the fifties, Dino's doin' everythin' right."

"So if it happens, maybe that'll bring the act back," I said.

"No, people will still come to see Dino," Jack said, "and they'll always come to see Frank, but the whole package has lost a lot of its' . . . spontaneity. People know what they're gonna get."

"So what's with Sammy and Jerry Lewis?"

"You know, Sammy's younger than Frank and Dean, but him and Jerry, they're about the same age. And they're friends. I think them bein' on stage together will be good."

"So this was your idea?"

He hesitated, then said, "Kinda."

"What do you mean, kinda?"

"I was talkin' to Frank and Dean, and it came up."

"Dean?" I asked. "I thought he and Jerry didn't get along?"

"Are you kiddin'?" he asked. "They don't see each other since their breakup, but they love each other."

"That's not what the tabloids say."

"You can't believe everythin' you read in the papers, Eddie," Jack said. "You oughtta know that."

"Is Dean still in town?" I knew he had just finished up in the Copa Room the night before. I hadn't had time to see the show, and we didn't get together afterward.

"Frank's not," Jack said, "but Dean's still here."

"On the golf course?"

"Exactly," Jack said. "And he wants to see you."

"Today?"

"Now!" Jack said. "He wants you to wait for him in the clubhouse."

"The Stardust?"

"Where else?"

I stood up.

"Am I off the clock?"

"No," Jack said, "you're gettin' paid."

One of my favorite things was to spend time with Dean and get paid for it.

\*\*\*

## That Old Dead Magic

I sat at the bar in the lounge of the Stardust Country Club, where I didn't need to show i.d. or anything to get in because I'd been there enough with Frank, Dean, Sammy, Joey and—going a little further back—Peter Lawford. They all had pretty good games, but it was general knowledge that Dino and Peter were the better players. Very often, during the Ocean's 11 days, they'd play at night, under the orange glow of the lights, with some high stakes involved.

I tried playing with them once or twice, but golf wasn't my game. So I preferred to sit in the lounge as they gathered around the piano and gave an impromptu show for the members.

The bartender put a beer down in front of me and said, "There you go, Eddie."

"Thanks, Gene," I said. He had been the bartender there for a lot of years, was now in his fifties with Marine style cut gray hair.

"You got any idea when Dino went out?"

"Early," Gene said, "real early. I think I heard him say somethin' about playin' thirty-six holes."

I winced and asked, "Who likes the game that much?"

"He does," Gene said. "So do Bing Crosby and Bob Hope, when they're in town."

"That many holes would wear the hell out of me," I said.

A member at the other end of the bar raised his hand, something Gene was always on the lookout for.

"Lemme know if you want anythin' else," he said.

"Sure, thanks."

"On Mr. Martin's tab," he added, with a smile.

"Natch."

I sipped, watching the members come and go from the golf course, and the parking lot. After about a half hour and two beers, Dino walked in, still wearing his gaudy golf sweater and slacks.

"Heya, pally," he said, slapping me on the back. "How's the boy?"

"I'm good, Dean," I said. "Sorry I didn't make your show last night."

"Sorry I didn't get a chance to call ya and invite ya," Dean said, with a smile. He was in his late forties now, but still as handsome as ever, and still sporting a full head of black hair—which, to me, looked like the natural color. Some show biz types used all kinds of hair dye and shoe polish to keep that color, but on Dean it looked genuine.

"Drink, Mr. Martin?" Gene came over and asked.

"Lemme have an orange juice, Gene and no lip about it."

"Comin' up."

Dean wasn't the boozer he pretended to be on stage. Most of the time that glass he held during his act had apple juice in it. Dean always said he hated apple juice. Oh, he drank, but this was too early for him to start, hence the O.J.

The thing that always startled me about Dean was that I was taller than he was. He stood five feet nine inches tall, but when he was on stage, he looked like he was over six feet. That might've been because Frank was only five-foot-seven and Sammy five-foot-six—even though Sammy always looked smaller because of the slight frame.

Gene brought Dino's juice over, then moved on down the bar. People looked at Dean as they went by, tried not to stare. Some exchanged a wave. But nobody bothered him, which was the way he wanted it, and the club people knew it. Nobody ever asked him to do a song, either. Once in a while he'd walk over to the piano on his own— or he and Frank would, when they were both there—but nobody ever requested it.

"Skoal," Dean said, clinking his juice glass against my beer glass.

I decided not to ask right away why he wanted to see me, but to let him get to it in his own time, so I asked. "How was your game today?"

"Perfect, as always," he said.

I waited, but he still didn't broach the subject. I wondered if he was going to make me ask.

## Chapter Two

"Jack told me about the failing attendance for the Summit," I said. "I find that hard to believe."

"Don't," Dean said. "It happens. We've had five years. That's a good run. Hell, I stuck it out with Jerry for ten."

"Was that why you broke up? People were getting tired of the act?"

"Hell, no," Dean said. "When Jerry and I parted ways, we still have two hundred and fifty million dollars in contracts."

"Jesus!" I said. "I didn't know that. And you walked away from it?"

"We both did," Dean said. "It was time. And I think we've both done pretty well on our own."

"I'd say so."

"And now it's time for us all to do the same," Dean said. "Frank's talkin' to the Sahara, I have meetings with the Riviera."

"You guys are gonna leave the Sands completely?" I asked.

"Not right away," Dean said. "It'll be little-by-little. We still owe Jack."

"So what's this thing with Sammy and Jerry?" I asked. "Jack said it was your idea."

He sipped his juice, swallowed and said, "Oh, not mine. It was Sam's."

"Really?"

"Yeah, he and Jerry are friends. They're only a year apart in age, and they have a lot in common. They both started out in this business as kids. Hell, they've got more in common than Jerry and I ever did."

I had never asked Dean about his break up with Jerry, but now Jack had mentioned it, and so did Dean. I figured why not, while the door was open?

"I thought you and Jerry didn't see each other or talk since the break up?" I said. "But Jack says you guys talk on the phone."

"We have," Dean said, "but we don't make a habit of it. Look, there's no bad blood, that's all newspaper guff. We don't hang around together because we've got nothin' to talk about. Back when we were partners, we talked about the act. That was it. He was always writing some new material, and tellin' me about it. Once we split, that was gone."

"So you don't spend time together because you literally have nothing to talk about?"

"If somethin' comes up, we discuss it," Dean said. "I mean, there's still some business. We did sixteen pictures together, after all. Seventeen if you count the walk on we did for Bob and Bing in The Road to Bali. That was enough."

"And they were all hits?"

"They were huge," Dean said, "but I hated every one of them. I just couldn't do it, anymore. And we both thought Hal Wallis was a putz. So, that was that."

There was a note of finality to that last remark, so I moved on and finally asked the question.

"So what did you want to see me about?"

"Oh, yeah." He finished his juice and put the empty down, shook his head at Gene that he didn't want a refill. "It's about Jack."

"Entratter? What about him?"

"I think he's going to take it hard," Dean said.

"The end of the Rat Pack, you mean?"

Dean winced. He and Frank never called it 'the Rat Pack.' That was the tabloids. To them it was 'The Summit.'

"Yeah," he said, "I think Jack's gonna take the blame for the whole thing fallin' apart."

I knew Jack well enough to understand.

"You're probably right."

"Well, I don't want him to feel that way," Dean said. "I'm gonna count on you to make sure he doesn't."

"Why me?"

"Because you're around him all the time, and we're not," Dean said. "Frank and I are both gonna count on you for this."

"Well, yeah, sure," I said. "I'll do my best."

He smiled broadly then and said, "That's what you always do, Eddie."

He stood up.

"What's goin' on?" I asked. "I mean . . . are things okay?"

He put his hand on my shoulder and said, "Things are goin' great, pally. My show starts in September. Meanwhile, I just did a movie with John Wayne that's comin' out, and I'm gonna be workin' on my first Matt Helm spy movie. And I've got a new album comin' out. So things are great. The Summit . . . that's just somethin' that's run its course."

"Oh," I said, "and I saw you on an episode of Rawhide."

"Aw, hell, that was fun, playin' a gunfighter. I love doin' Westerns. I've done two with Duke, and I'm gonna do more. And Frank's got a bunch of new movies comin', and a new album, too. I'm gonna have him on my show." He squeezed my shoulder. "Life couldn't be better, pally."

I stood up, as well.

"Well, I'm glad to hear it. How's Jeannie?"

"She's great, and so are the kids."

"When are you leavin'?" I asked.

"Flyin' out tomorrow."

"Give her my best, will you?"

"I sure will."

He gave me a hug, which surprised me. It was so quick I didn't have time to react.

"But first I'm gonna go and shoot a few more holes," he said. "See ya, Clyde."

"See ya, Dino."

As he left the clubhouse, members looked over at me, wondering who this guy was that Dean Martin hugged?

## Chapter Three

I drove back to the Sands, marquees along the strip announcing Steve & Eydie, Red Skelton and Jack Jones at different hotels. Pulling into the Sands parking lot, I took another look at the marquee. Sammy and Jerry's name were the same size, but Sam's was on the marquee first. Judging by what I'd heard over the years about Jerry Lewis' ego, that surprised me. If he and Sammy were friends though, they must've worked it out between themselves.

I had been off for two days at Jack Entratter's insistence, since working two weeks straight before. That's what happens when the high rollers—the "whales"—keep coming and making demands. When I'd gone home two days ago, Dean's name had been up on that marquee. Now it was gone, replaced with Sammy's and Jerry Lewis'.

I parked behind the building and used a rear entrance to go inside. Now that I had satisfied both Jack and Dean, I still had two whales I had to see to that day before I could stop and have either a late lunch or—depending on how hard they were to satisfy—an early dinner.

***

As it turned out, both of my high rollers wanted a high stakes poker game, so I was able to satisfy them both by putting them in the same room, at the same table. One of them was an attractive woman in her early fifties, who somehow managed to have her hand on my butt every few minutes. She kept herself in good shape, so I figured if I had to, I'd have to put up with her groping.

The things I do for high rollers.

Then I went to lunch in the Garden Cafe.

\*\*\*

My private eye buddy, Danny Bardini, was waiting for me in a booth. Usually when we had lunch together, we'd do it just a few feet from his office on Fremont Street, in the downstairs coffee shop in Binion's Horseshoe. But this time Danny said he wanted a Garden Café lunch, so I agreed to meet him there.

"There you are," he said, when I slid into the booth across from him. "I'm starving."

"You should've ordered," I said.

"Never mind, just get the waitress over here. Use your influence."

He said that because the café was crowded, and the girls were running back and forth, with tables of people waving frantically for their attention.

So I used my influence, waved my arm once, and one of the girls hurried over.

"Hi, Eddie," blonde Virginia said. "Crazy day. What'll ya have?"

"Thanks Gina. Just bring me a burger platter and a beer."

"Right. And you, handsome?" she asked, giving Danny the full benefit of a beautiful smile. Gina was only working as a waitress until they had room for her in the chorus line. She had small, but firm, high breasts and legs that didn't stop. She'd be dancing before long.

"I'll have the meat loaf, doll, and a brew," Danny said.

"You got it, sexy," she said, and hurried off.

"Wow," Danny said, watching her rump twitch as she walked away.

"Enjoy while you can," I said. "Soon you'll have to pay to see that ass."

"I figured she was a dancer," he said. "With those legs, what else could she be?"

Gina returned with two mugs of beer, then hurried away again. Several of the diners around us were glaring at us, wondering how we rated.

17

"What's on your mind, Danny?" I asked.

"Why does something have to be on my mind?"

"Because we're not in the Horseshoe Coffee Shop, and you're eating meat loaf."

"As I remember it, the meat loaf here is pretty good."

"Everything here's pretty good." Danny's Brooklyn accent was almost as slight as mine. We'd both been in Vegas long enough for that. Other people claimed to be able to hear it in us, but we didn't even hear it in each other. Admittedly, mine gets thicker when I get agitated.

"Come on, what are you working on?" I asked.

"Okay, yeah," he said, "I'm working on something, and I need a girl."

"For what?"

"Bait."

"Why come to me?" I asked.

"Because the Sands has what I need, in spades," he said. "I need a hot dolly with a beautiful face and legs that don't quit."

As if on cue, Gina came back carrying two plates. She set them down, gave Danny a broad smile and said, "You need anything else, handsome, you let me know." She looked at me and said, "Eddie."

"Thanks, Gin."

As she walked away with both of us watching Danny said, "You wouldn't be making it with that, wouldja Eddie?"

"If only," I said. "No, I'm celibate, these days."

"Well sure," he said, "When you've slept with Judith Campbell and Ava Gardner it's kind of hard to find something to match them."

"Hey," I said, "A gentleman never tells."

"Still not admitting you slept with Ava, huh?"

"Why do you need a girl for bait?"

Thankfully, he let go of the Ava thing. I still wanted to keep the fact that I'd slept with her from Frank.

"I'm trying to nail this scumbag who's beating on women, and I need a piece of bait that he won't be able to resist."

"So you thought a Sands showgirl would be perfect."

"Can you think of something more perfect?" he asked. "Maybe a Riviera showgirl?"

"They've got good ones," I said, "but they can't match ours."

"That's what I was thinking," he said, putting ketchup on his meat loaf.

I did the same to my burger and fries, but that made sense. He was sloppy about it and got some on his mashed potatoes and gravy.

"But I need something else from you," he said.

"And what's that?"

He chewed, swallowed and said, "Jerry."

# Chapter Four

"I need a backbreaker I can trust," he said.

"All the way from Brooklyn?"

"I also need a face nobody around here's gonna know," Danny said.

I shrugged.

"Why are you asking me?" I said. "You know 'im. Call 'im yourself."

"I just wanted to check with you first," Danny said. "I didn't want to step on anyone's toes."

"No toes, here," I said.

"Good."

We tucked into our meals and finished them in record time, because the Garden Café had a line of people waiting to get in. Gina brought our check and as I grabbed it Danny asked her, "Can I call you?"

She wrote her number on a napkin, handed it to him and said, "Anytime, handsome."

Danny had a great lunch. He got his meat loaf, his bait, and the okay to call his muscle.

He was one happy shamus.

\*\*\*

I was crossing the lobby of the hotel to stop at the front desk, as I usually did each day to see if I had any messages, when I saw Jack Entratter get off the elevator. I changed direction and intercepted him.

"What's up?" Jack asked. "I'm on my way to a meeting."

"Just wanted to let you know I talked to Dean," I said. "Seems he's a little worried about you."

"Me? Why?"

"He's afraid you'll think that the lack of draws for the Rat Pack is somehow your fault."

"Why wouldn't it be my fault?" Entratter asked. "I'm in charge, ain't I?"

"Look, Jack—"

"And why's he talkin' to you about me?" Entratter went on. He was this close to being enraged, and if we hadn't been in a public place, he might've blown. Instead, he leaned in and growled, "You tell that dago crooner to mind his own business."

As he stormed off, I stood there and wondered how I would put that to Dino?

# Chapter Five

Dean had to leave the next day, rather than stay for Sammy and Jerry's show. I think if it had just been Sam, he would have stayed.

I didn't see Entratter the rest of the day after the meeting in the lobby of the hotel, and I decided not to go and see him the next morning. I'd just wait until we crossed paths under normal conditions.

I saw to the needs of my high rollers in the morning (not the female, as she slept in after a late night) and after a lone lunch at the bar in the Silver Queen, staring at the mural behind the bar, I headed for the front desk to check for messages. The high rollers didn't like it when it took me too long to return their calls.

But there were none from my whales, the only message I had was from an unexpected source—Sammy Davis Jr. It simply said: "Call me, please."

I hadn't gotten as close with Sam as I had with Frank and Dino, but I liked him. I wasn't about to make him wait for me to call back, so I got a phone from the desk clerk and had the operator put me through to Sam's suite.

"Hey, Eddie, my man," Sammy said, "thanks for callin' me back, man."

"What's up, Sam? The suite okay?"

"It's fine, man, it's a gas, as usual," Sammy said. "But . . . I've got somethin' else on my mind. D'ya think you can come up here and talk about it?"

"Sure, Sam," I said. "I'll be right up."

"Groovy," he said, and hung up.

Sammy had a habit of trying to go with current trends, to keep himself relevant, I guess. So he'd say things like "groovy" and "far out." I was afraid he was going to start wearing psychedelic shirts and chains (not realizing that in two years' time he'd be doing just that on TV's Laugh-In.) But so far, on stage, he was sticking to tuxedoes.

I hung up and took the elevator to Sam's floor. I didn't know if Jerry Lewis was on the same floor or not. I thought, for the moment, that I'd leave Jerry's comfort to Jack Entratter, until I heard different.

I knocked on the door and Sammy swung it open in seconds.

"Hey, Eddie!" He grabbed my hand and bumped shoulders with me. "Come on in, man."

I entered and closed the door behind me while he headed for the bar.

"Ya wanna drink?" he asked.

"A little early in the day for me, Sam."

"I got coffee," he said.

"Oh, then sure, I'll have a cup. Black, no sugar."

"Groovy," he said, and I tried not to twitch.

I walked to the bar and took a stool, and he put a cup of coffee in front of me. I didn't know if he'd been drinking, but right then he poured himself a cup of coffee.

"Good java, man," he said. "The Sands always has the best, huh?"

"Of everything, Sam," I said, "that's why you're here."

"Touché," he said, and toasted me with his cup.

"So what's up, Sam?" I asked. "I gotta say, when I got back from my days off, I was surprised to see your name on the marquee with Jerry Lewis."

"Yeah, I know," Sammy said. "The Summit days are winding down, I guess. I thought maybe doin' somethin' with Jerry might liven things up again."

"If you don't mind him steppin' on your songs," I said, then realized how I sounded. "Sorry, sorry, I just— are we bein' candid, here?"

"If we are," he said, "I'll cut out the 'groovy' stuff."

"Good deal," I said. "Between you and me, I was never a Martin and Lewis fan. Didn't get their act, and didn't like the films. Oh, I know they're both talented, and since they split, I understand both of their popularity. It's just . . . the handsome singer/monkey stuff I never got, you know?"

"I getcha," he said. "Jerry's an acquired taste, I guess. But him and me, we got an awful lot in common."

"So I heard."

"Oh? From who?"

"I saw Dean at the golf club yesterday," I said.

"He mentioned me and Jerry?"

"No, I brought it up," I said, "and he told me how much you guys had in common. He thinks you and Jerry make sense."

"Hey, that's great!" Sammy said. "I wasn't sure whether or not I should be askin' his permission, you know?"

"I get that," I replied, "but he doesn't have a problem with it."

"Dino's a great guy!" Sammy gushed. "I guess that's why Frank thinks of him as a best friend."

"You're probably right." I decided to let Sammy get to the point all on his own, so I sipped my coffee. He was right. The Sands had the best coffee in town.

"Okay," he said, finally, "I guess you're wonderin' why I asked you to come up here."

"You guess right," I said. "I figure you've got a problem."

"I do, but it's not my problem, really," Sammy said, "it's Jerry's. I think he needs help."

"With what?'

"I probably shouldn't be tellin' you this," Sammy said, "but I think Jerry's gonna try to kill somebody."

# Chapter Six

"Wait," I said. "He's—he's a funnyman. Why would he want to kill someone?"

"He's a funnyman on stage," Sammy said, "and in the movies. Other than that, Jerry's very serious about what he does."

"Serious enough to kill someone?"

"I hope not, but—"

"But what?" I asked. "Who's he want to kill?"

"That I don't know."

"Then what makes you think there even is someone?"

"Just some things he said," Sammy explained. "We had a few drinks one night, and Jerry doesn't usually drink. He got drunk, started talking about someone from his past who had showed up recently, someone he was . . . gonna get rid of."

"By killing?"

"He didn't actually say that."

"Okay, so what if someone from his past turned up and is blackmailing him? Maybe he just plans to pay them off."

"I hope that's what it is," Sammy said, "but I'm also hoping you can find out."

"Me? Why me?"

"Because according to Frank and Dean, you're the guy."

Not that again, I thought.

"And I've been around you long enough to know that it's true," Sammy went on. "If anybody can get to the bottom of this, it's you."

"Is that why you brought Jerry here to perform at the Sands with you?"

"It didn't take much convincing," Sam said, "but yeah."

"Sammy, he doesn't even know me," I said. "What makes you think he'd talk to me?"

Sammy leaned his elbows on the bar, grinned at me and raised his eyebrows.

"I'm gonna introduce the two of you," he said. "The rest is gonna be up to you." He poked me in the chest. "You're gonna dig and dig the way you do, and come up with the answer. I know you are."

"How long are you and Jerry booked in here for?" I asked.

"Three days," Sammy said, "unless we get held over."

"And this is all based on one drunken conversation one night?" I asked.

"You didn't see him, Eddie," Sammy said, straightening up. "His eyes, they were . . . dead. Jerry's eyes are never that way. Something's goin' on with him."

"Okay," I said, "when do I meet him?"

"Come to the show tonight," Sammy said. "I'll make the introductions and you can take it from there."

"I hope you're right about this, Sam," I said. "I hope he needs help, and I won't just be buttin' into his business."

"As long as you can convince him that it involves casino business," Sammy said, "you can ask him whatever you want."

"You better be right."

He walked me to the door, his hand on my shoulder.

"Actually," he said, as I stepped out into the hall, "I'm hopin' I'm wrong."

As the door closed, I thought, so am I.

***

As I left the elevator down on the lobby floor, one of the desk clerks walked up to me with a message.

"It came in just as you left the desk earlier," he said, handing it to me

It was from Big Jerry Epstein, from Brooklyn. It said, simply, "Call me back."

I went right to a house pay phone and put the call in.

"Hey, Mr. G.!" he exclaimed. "Thanks for gettin' back to me so quick."

"What's on your mind, big guy?" I asked, even though I thought I knew.

"I got a call from your buddy, Bardini," Jerry explained. "He said he needs some help and wants me to come out."

"Did he say what for, exactly?"

"No, just that he'd send me a ticket—which he done, already."

"So what's the problem?"

"I just wanted to check with you and make sure it's okay if I help him out."

"Sure, it is, Jerry," I said. "That is, if you don't mind doin' it."

"Naw, I don't mind," Jerry said, "as long as you don't mind."

I felt like we were starting an Abbott and Costello routine.

"Jerry," I said, "you do whatever you feel is right. I'll be glad to see you."

"Well, I like the bum ya know?"

"I know."

"So, I guess I'll come. Can I stay there?"

"Sure," I said, "your room is ready."

## Chapter Seven

I went to the Sam & Jerry Show that night.

That wasn't the name they chose. They were introduced as an evening with Sammy Davis Jr. and Jerry Lewis. I watched from the back of the room as they tried to reenact some of the old Martin & Lewis routines, and sing some songs together. Then Lewis left the stage so Sammy could sing solo, but, after one or two, Jerry kept interrupting him with his clown act. The audience laughed, but the whole thing made me uncomfortable. I was actually glad when it was over.

As the crowd filed out, I made my way to the front of the room, and then back to the dressing rooms. Sammy was talking to some reporters in the hall, but Jerry Lewis was nowhere to be seen. Then Sammy spotted me and broke away from the press.

"I'm glad you're here," he said. "What'd you think of the show?"

"You don't want to know," I said.

"Why?" he asked. "The crowd lapped it up."

"That's what's important, right?"

"Eddie—"

"Let it go, Sam," I said. "Where's Lewis?"

"In his dressing room," Sammy said. "He didn't want to talk to the press. He left that to me. Come on, I'll introduce you."

I followed, but I wasn't looking forward to this.

We stopped in front of Lewis' dressing room door and Sammy knocked.

"I said no press!" a voice called from inside. I didn't recognize it.

"It's me, Jerry . . . Sammy."

"Oh, hey, come on in."

As Sammy started to open the door, I grabbed his arm.

"Is that him?"

"Yeah," Sammy said, "that's his real voice. You know, when he's not doing that high-pitched kid thing. Haven't you seen his movies?"

"To tell you the truth no," I said. "I've always been put off by grown men acting like kids."

"You really aren't the audience for him, are ya?" Sam asked.

He turned the doorknob and we went in.

Jerry Lewis was sitting in a chair in front of a dressing table mirror, staring at himself. Now that he wasn't on stage, he even looked different, and suddenly I knew what had been making me so uncomfortable. He started out with Dino when he was nineteen, playing a silly kid. He kept it up for years, until he was still doing it in his thirties. Now he was a man of almost forty, and I'd found it really off-putting for him to try playing the goofy, zany, high-voiced kid again.

"Hey, Sam," he said.

"Jerry," Sammy said, "this is my friend, Eddie Gianelli. The cats call him Eddie G."

He stood up and I was surprised to find that he was a six-footer.

"How are you," he asked, extending his hand. "How'd you like the show?"

I looked at Sammy. Jerry noticed and frowned.

"What?" he asked.

"You can tell him the truth," Sammy said. "What's the point of lyin'?"

"You didn't like it?" Jerry asked me.

"It just didn't have the same . . . energy as you and Dean had," I said.

Jerry looked at Sam, who shrugged.

"He's right," Jerry said. "You know, I felt like I was forcing it."

"Yeah, but the crowd ate it up," Sammy said. "They laughed their asses off."

"Yeah," Jerry said, "at the funny monkey boy."

"Hey," Sammy corrected, "the black Jew and the monkey."

"Right, right," Jerry said. "Hey, thanks for talking to the press, Sam."

"No problem, but now I gotta go to my dressing room and get cleaned up," Sammy said. "You mind if I leave Eddie here, Jerry?"

"No, not at all," Jerry said. "He's honest. I like that."

"Cool," Sammy said. "I'll be back in fifteen or twenty. You wanna go out and get a bite with us?" he asked me.

"Sure, Sam."

"Okay," Sammy said, "I won't be long."

He left the dressing room, leaving me alone with Jerry Lewis. Only this wasn't any Jerry Lewis I had ever seen. He was older, more serious, with a well-modulated voice and an educated way of speaking. No sign of the high-pitched funnyman, at all.

"I'll get the rest of this gunk off my face," Jerry said. "Go ahead."

He sat and talked while he wiped his face.

"I'd forgotten how much more of this junk you use on stage."

"Has it been a while since you've been on stage?"

"Oh, yeah," Jerry said, "been making movies for a long time, now." He turned and looked at me. "Have you seen my movies?"

"Hasn't everybody?" I asked. "From My Friend Irma to the Disorderly Orderly."

He turned back to the mirror.

"Yeah, those sixteen films I made with Dean— seventeen if you count the walk on in Hope and Crosby's Road to Bali . . . man, Dean hated those movies."

I knew that. And, to tell the truth, I hadn't seen The Disorderly Orderly, I just knew it was his most recent.

"Can't say I blame him, either," Jerry said. "People never gave Dean his due when we were together, you know? It was Jerry this, Jerry that, Jerry's so funny . . . if it was up to me, if our roles were reversed, I would've quit five years earlier than he did."

He turned in his chair again.

"You know, I was only as funny as I was because I had him to play off of. He had amazing comic timing— still does."

I wondered why he was telling me all this?

"But why am I tellin' you all this?" he said, as if reading my mind. He looked at me in the mirror. "Do people usually pour their hearts out to you? Tell secrets?"

"Sometimes," I said, "but usually it's women."

Jerry laughed.

"Well," he said, "whatever it is, I think I'm going to keep the rest of my secrets to myself, for now."

"Good idea."

# Chapter Eight

A Sands limo took us to the Golden Steer steakhouse on West Sahara, where Frank had a private booth he sat in every time he went there.

"Mr. Sinatra's booth? Of course, Mr. G.," the maître d' said when I inquired. "I mean, as long as Mr. Sinatra isn't in town."

"Take my word for it, Julius, he's not."

"Then this way, please. I'd be happy to seat you and Mr. Davis and Mr. Lewis."

We drew looks crossing the floor, and a comment or two. Sammy waved, I greeted one or two people I knew, and Jerry stared straight ahead. I was starting to wonder if Jerry was the unfunniest funnyman when he wasn't on stage? Buddy Hackett, Shecky Greene, Rickles, even Joey Bishop, they were funny as hell on or off stage. Jerry Lewis' serious demeanor was a shock to me.

We sat, ordered drinks and steak dinners, while Sammy and Jerry talked a bit about the show.

"I think the mistake," Jerry said, "was in trying to do Martin and Lewis. That stuff is from the old days. We need to do something new."

"And how do we get somethin' new ready in time for tomorrow night?" Sammy asked.

"I'll write something tonight," Jerry assured him. "Then run it by you tomorrow."

"Run it by me?" Sammy asked. "No rehearsal? I'm not Dean Martin, you know."

"I know," Jerry said. "That's the point. Dean was a sponge. I showed him something once and he got it. Don't worry, Sam. We'll have it in time."

After that, Sammy started talking to me, asking what I was up to, when I had last seen Frank and Dean, what was going on behind the scenes at the Sands. Jerry ate his steak and listened. I had the feeling he could have repeated everything back at a later date, word for word.

After cheesecake and coffee, I got the bill and settled it. Sammy and Jerry resisted, but then gave in when I said, "On the Sands. We take care of our performers."

The limo took us back to the Sands and I asked, "Nightcap?"

"Sure, why not?" Sam said.

"I've got to get to my suite and start writing," Jerry said. "Another time, maybe. Goodnight."

As Jerry walked off across the lobby to the elevators, I turned to Sammy and asked, "Who was that masked man?"

"Let's get that drink," he said.

\*\*\*

Once we were set up with drinks in the lounge, I said to Sammy, "That's not any Jerry Lewis I've ever seen before."

"That's because he's not makin' a movie, or on stage," Sammy said. "There are no cameras."

"So that's the real Jerry Lewis?" I asked. "So serious?"

"Jerry had a painful childhood," Sammy said.

"And he keeps all the pain inside, being serious all the time?" I asked.

"That's just it," Sammy said. "The pain comes out in his comedy, in the manic performances he gives. All that high-pitched 'Laaaaadeeee' stuff. That's the release."

"It's just . . . strange to see this version of him," I said. "And while you were gone, he spoke about Dean with such . . . reverence."

"He loves the guy," Sammy said.

"Well, I'd ask why they broke up, but I've heard it now from Jerry and from Dean."

"They had to get away from each other and be their own men," Sammy said, "build their own careers."

"Well, it seems to me Dean's come away with the better end of the deal," I said. "He's had hit records, and smash movies, and now he'll probably have a hit TV show."

"Well," Sammy said, "if I'm going to play devil's advocate, Jerry hasn't done bad, either. He's had hit movies, and records, he's an actor, a director, a writer . . . and he has the telethon."

"Yeah," I said, "but calling Jerry Lewis an actor, that's like callin' a monkey an actor. Dean has done some serious roles since they broke up, and his records have sold millions of copies. Jerry does records where he yells 'Laaaaaadeeee' and people laugh."

"This is an argument that could go on forever," Sammy said, "and my problem is, they're both my friends."

"I understand that."

"Eddie, I just need you to help Jerry," Sammy said, "not like him."

"I don't dislike him," I said, "I don't know him well enough for that. I'm just not a big fan of what he does. But if he needs help, I'm here."

"Well," Sammy said, "I've put you together, now I'm hopin' you can do the rest."

"Sammy, I'll do what I can," I promised.

"I can't ask for more than that," he said. "I'm gonna turn in now. I'll see you tomorrow."

"Goodnight, Sam."

# Chapter Nine

I drove to McCarran Airport the next day to pick up Big Jerry. As usual, he showed up with one bag, while wearing a houndstooth sports jacket. And he drove my Caddy to the Sands.

"What's this problem the dick has that he needs me for?" Jerry asked.

"I don't know the details," I said. "He just asked my permission to call you."

"Really?" he said. "Your permission?"

"Well, no, not really," I said. "I think he was just bouncing the possibility off me. I told him to go ahead, if he needed you, you'd decide whether or not to come."

"Why wouldn't I?" he asked. "I love Vegas."

I noticed that Big Jerry had kept off the weight he'd lost after being diagnosed with diabetes.

"How are you feelin', these days?" I asked.

"Hungry all the time," he said, "but I know what you mean. I've been keepin' my sugar under control—most days."

"That's good."

"But I could still go for some pancakes."

"You got it."

\*\*\*

In the Garden Café he ordered a short stack. I had skipped breakfast to pick him up, and I had the same, so as not to rub it in.

"You don't need to do that on my account," he said, after we ordered.

"That's okay," I lied. "I had some toast before I picked you up."

When the waitress came with our orders Jerry asked, "Can I get some extra butter?"

She was a middle-aged woman I knew as Bea, who gave him a motherly look and said, "I'll bring some more."

"Since I can't use syrup anymore, I just douse my pancakes with plenty of butter."

"But is that good for you?" I asked.

"I don't know," he admitted. "I ain't asked my doctor about that . . . yet."

She returned with a smile and set some extra butter on the table.

"Let me know if you need anything else, hon," she said to Jerry. She looked at me. "You okay, Eddie?"

"Fine, Bea. Where's Gina today? She's usually on this shift."

"She took a few days off for some reason," Bea said. "Nobody knows why. Something personal, I guess."

"Okay, thanks."

As Bea walked away and Jerry smeared butter on his pancakes he asked, "This Gina's a girlfriend, Mr. G.?"

"No, nothin' like that. Danny said he also needs a girl as bait . . . must be the same case he needs you for."

"That don't sound good," he said. "Why would he want a waitress as bait?"

"Gina's a dancer," I said. "She's workin' here while she waits for somethin' to open up at one of the hotels."

"So she's good-lookin'?"

"Very," I said. "She's got the long legs and everything."

"I guess I better give the shamus a call after we eat," he said.

Jerry rarely—if ever—called Danny by name. He was either "the dick," or "the shamus" or "the gumshoe." But I knew they liked each other.

While we ate, I told Jerry about Sammy Davis and Jerry Lewis being in the Copa Room.

"Why's Mr. Davis doin' that?" he asked. "Where's the other guys from the Rat Pack?"

"Apparently," I said, "they're all doin' their own shows at other hotels. I've been told they're not packin' them in here like they used to."

"That's too bad," he said. "I really liked that show they did—once they got rid of that limey, I mean."

Peter Lawford didn't appeal to everyone. I never liked him much, neither did Jerry, and he was on the outs permanently with Frank. I thought Sammy kept in touch with him, but I didn't know about Dean and Joey.

When we arrived at the Sands, we had gone right to the Garden Room, so once we had eaten Jerry said, "I better go up to my room and give the gumshoe a call."

"I had your bag taken up," I told him.

"Thanks, Mr. G."

We left the restaurant together and walked out to the hotel lobby.

"I've gotta go to work, Jerry. You'll be able to find me if you need me."

"And I guess if you need me you can call the P.I. or check my room."

"Would you want to see the show tonight?"

"I wouldn't mind seein' Mr. Davis, but I ain't crazy about the other guy," he said. "I never knew why Mr. Martin thought he needed him. That crazy stuff he does gives me the willies."

"Then afterwards we'll catch up," I said, and we went our separate ways.

# Chapter Ten

I let Big Jerry take the Caddy to meet with Danny, while I went about my day. A couple of my high rollers wanted tickets to the Copa Room to see Sammy and Jerry, so I made it happen. I imagined Jerry Lewis was spending the morning briefing Sammy on whatever he had written the night before. I knew he had done the same kind of thing with Dean, sometime briefing Dean on the new material on the way back from the golf course. Then they'd go on stage and Dean wouldn't miss a beat. I wondered if Dean was going to do his own show the same way, with hardly any rehearsal?

Frank had been that way when they were in Vegas shooting Ocean's 11. He insisted everybody get it right the first time, because they were only going to do one take. That movie got made in record time and, luckily, they were all pros, from Angie Dickinson to Richard Conte, Caesar Romero and Akim Tamiroff.

I was walking past the Garden Room when I heard the woman's voice.

"Oh, Eddie."

I turned. It was my lady high roller. Her name was Mrs. Kaufman. She came to Vegas several times a year, without her husband. She was in her early fifties, twenty-five years younger than her rich husband. She kept herself in good shape, with tennis and the gym. I could see what a looker she had been when she was younger. Now she was trying to hang on to her looks. She kept her hair blonde, not allowing any grey to show, and used lots of makeup to cover crow's feet at the corners of her eyes, and the wrinkles at the corners of her mouth.

"I've been looking for you, darling," she said, sliding her arm into mine. "Walk with me?"

"Of course, Mrs. Kaufman."

"Eddie, I come here a lot, and I've asked you to call me Grace."

"Oh, right, sorry, Grace."

"Now what have you been doing, avoiding me? I'd like you to come to my room this evening."

"Is there a problem?"

"Yes," she said, "I need sex, and I don't want to pay for it."

"Grace—"

"Come on," she said, "I've been subtle with you, and you don't take the hints. Don't you like me?"

"Of course I do," I said. "You're a lovely woman—"

"I know I'm a little older than you, but not by much. And I can assure you, you'll love it." She lowered her voice. "I'm very good."

"I'm sure you are," I said, "but I could get fired for sleeping with a guest."

"I won't tell if you don't." She disengaged her arm and patted my cheek. "You know my room number." She leaned in closer and whispered, "And I'm *very*, very good."

"Grace—" I started, but she walked off, her heels making a staccato beat on the floor, until she reached the rug on the casino floor.

Grace Kaufman was an attractive woman, and, if she wasn't a guest, maybe I would have considered her offer. It had been a dry spell for me, of late.

After all, nobody had to know . . .

\*\*\*

I spent the rest of the afternoon putting out fires that kept popping up, one after the other. There was a fist fight between two high rollers, which had to be broken up without alienating either party. Jack Entratter got real upset when our high rollers decided to go elsewhere to lose their fortunes.

My responsibilities at the Sands kept increasing, somewhat unofficially. There was even a problem in the kitchen that I was called on to fix. The job actually fell under the purview of the general manager of the hotel, but that position happened to be vacant, at the moment.

Maybe I needed—or deserved—a raise.

# Chapter Eleven

I didn't know how Sammy expected me to get Jerry Lewis to talk to me. It seemed pretty obvious from our first meeting that Jerry and I weren't going to click—at least, not in the way I had done with the Rat Pack guys. I considered all four—Frank, Dino, Sammy and Joey—my friends, and both Frank and Dean my *good* friends. Right now, Jerry and I were acquaintances, and I didn't know how that was going to change.

I thought about asking Dean to get Jerry to talk to me, but if they didn't talk very much, then how would that work? I had to discuss options with Sammy, so I called his room. There was no answer, which made me think he was either in Jerry's room, or at the pool.

Sammy liked going to the pool, even though he didn't go in the water. There was still some resistance from hotel owners to allow blacks into the big hotels. Even the entertainers, like Sammy, Nat Cole, Redd Foxx, had to stay in hotels off the strip. The only reason Sam got a suite at the Sands was because Frank insisted on it. He told Entratter that if Sam didn't get a room, there would be no show. Entratter had to give in.

So Sammy would get into a bathing suit, walk down to the pool, and scare all the white guests by pretending he was going to dive into the water. Then he'd sit in a chaise lounge, have a drink, and go back inside, having given everybody a good scare. One time he was feeling particularly playful—or maybe it was resentful—and he actually stuck one toe into the pool. The complaints poured in and Jack Entratter had no choice but to drain the pool and refill it.

I checked the pool and there was no sign of Sammy, just the happy people splashing around to their heart's content because no evil black man had polluted the water. I wondered if the same thing would have happened if Lola Falana had walked to the pool in her bikini and stuck her toe in? The women probably would have complained, while the men crowded around her.

I went back inside, thought about calling Jerry Lewis' room, then decided, why not? If Sammy was there maybe I'd go on up and bond with the funnyman.

Jerry answered his phone on the fifth ring.

"I said I didn't want any calls while I'm working!" he shouted.

"Oh, hey, sorry Jerry," I said, sensing that we still hadn't bonded, "I was lookin' for Sam. Oh, it's Eddie G."

"Hold on," he snapped. He must have put his hand over the receiver, because all I heard was some muffled conversation, and then Sammy came on.

"Sorry about that Eddie," Sam said. "Jerry gets that way when he works. What can I do for you?"

"Invite me up."

He lowered his voice.

"Why?"

"I need an excuse to see Jerry," I said. "How else am I gonna get closer to him?"

"Okay," Sammy said, "give me a sec."

More muffled conversation, some of which sounded like it may have been an argument, then Sammy came back on.

"Come on up, Eddie," Sammy said, loud enough for Jerry to hear, "and bring some Luckies."

"Got it," I said.

I went to the gift shop, got a carton of Lucky Strikes, and went up.

***

Sammy opened the door and said, "Hey, Eddie. Come on in, man," with forced good humor.

I entered, saw Jerry sitting on the sofa, leaning over the coffee table, writing something. He was wearing a blue short-sleeved, button down shirt, a pair of chinos, and slippers with no socks. Sammy had a colorful shirt on, bare-chested under it, a pair of shorts, and sandals on his small feet. He looked like he had just come from, or was going to, the pool.

"Here's your Luckies," I said, handing him the carton.

"Thanks. You want a drink, man?"

"Yeah," I said. "Something with orange juice."

"One screwdriver comin' up."

I hated screwdrivers, but I didn't want anything strong at the moment.

Jerry kept his head down and kept writing, so I followed Sam to the bar.

He slid a glass over to me and said in a low voice, "Give him some time, he'll come around."

"Sure he will."

"Sam," Jerry said, "let's try this now. Eddie can be our audience."

"Sure," Sammy said, "that's cool." He gave me a look, then moved out from behind the bar and joined Jerry by the sofa.

I watched them work and got the feeling this was nothing like when Jerry and Dean did it. It seemed to me Jerry and Sammy argued more than anything else.

"You know," Jerry said, at one point, "I only ever had to show Dean somethin' one time." He held a forefinger out to Sammy to illustrate his point.

"I know that, Jer," Sammy said, "but in case you haven't noticed, I ain't Dean."

"Oh, I've noticed," Jerry assured him.

"What's that supposed to mean?"

"Jesus," I called out, "is this how the two of you work?"

They both turned and looked at me.

"Just bicker and fight?" I asked. "How the hell does anythin' get done?"

I decided to give Sammy a hint and see if he took it.

"Come on, Sam," I said, "you're bein' unreasonable."

He stared at me.

"Jerry's just tryin' to get you to focus," I went on. "You know how hard it is for you to do that."

"Me?" Sammy said. "I have trouble focusin'?"

"Why don't you take a walk and cool down," I suggested. "Then, when you come back, you'll be able to get some work done."

"Cool down," Sammy said, finally understanding that we were playing good cop/bad cop. And I was supposed to be the good cop. "Yeah, that's what I'll do. Take a walk and cool down. Maybe I'll go down to the pool and give them a real scare. I'll jump in. That'll cool me down."

He turned toward the door and stormed out, slamming it behind him.

Leaving me alone with Jerry Lewis.

## Chapter Twelve

I looked at Jerry and said, "You want a drink? Coffee?"

He stared back at me, then said, "Yeah, somethin' with orange juice."

"Screwdriver?" I asked.

"No," he said, "just orange juice."

I got behind the bar, and he walked over.

"Here you go," I said, sliding a glass of O. J. over to him. "Excitable little cuss, ain't he?"

"Sam's okay," Lewis said, picking up the juice. "I'm just used to Dean."

"Still?" I asked. "After all this time?"

"Seems like yesterday, to me. We were a hell of a team," he said. "I'm not being fair to Sam."

"I guess I should've taken his side, then."

"No, no," Lewis said, "don't take sides, Eddie. I know you're friends with Sam, but so am I. Let's just all . . . stay friends."

Had he really said that?

"I should let the two of you work, then," I said, leaving my glass on the bar and coming around. "But since it's my job to see to the needs of the Sands' special guests, let me know if you need anything, Jerry."

"Anything?" he said.

"A game?"

"I don't gamble."

"Tickets?"

"Not interested in other shows."

"Reservations?"

"I like room service."

"Help, then."

"Help?"

"Yeah," I said. "From time to time I've helped the guys with some problems."

"I heard that," he said, "from Sam. You're *the* guy in Vegas, he says."

"If you've got a problem in Vegas, yeah, I can help," I said. "Sometimes my help extends to places like L.A., Chicago, New York . . ."

"You're that connected?" he asked.

"My connections have connections," I told him.

He studied me for a moment, his mouth moving as if he was sucking on something, then said, "I'll keep that in mind. If you see Sam, send him back up, will you?"

"Will do."

I left him at the bar with his orange juice and exited the suite.

\*\*\*

I found Sammy waiting in the lobby as I got off the elevator.

"Well?" he asked.

"He wants you to go back up," I said. "Seems he thinks he was unfair to you."

"What about . . ." He looked around, lowered his voice. ". . . you know, the other thing?"

"Nothing yet," I said, "but I let him know that I'm available to help . . . my friends."

"Then I'll reinforce that," he said. "I better get back up there, though. We've got a show to do tonight. Will you be there?"

"I don't think so," I said. "I've got other things to do while I wait for Jerry Lewis to come around. Are you sure about this?"

"No, I'm not," Sammy said, his voice rising, "that's why I need you."

# Chapter Thirteen

I was sitting in the Silver Queen Lounge at a time when I knew Sammy and Jerry were walking out onto the stage in the Copa Room. I wondered if the new aspects of their act would go over big with the crowd.

I was relaxing, having put out all the fires I needed to for one day, including Sammy's. The high rollers were all in their games and would be deep into the night. Hopefully, everyone would get along and there'd be no calls for me.

The bartender came over with the phone and said, "For you, Eddie."

"Thanks. Hello?"

"Eddie, pal," Frank's voice said. There was no mistaking those dulcet tones. "What're you doing right now?"

"Havin' a drink and takin' a breath," I said. "Where are you, Frank?"

"I'm at the Sahara," he said. "They're tryin' to convince me to play here as a permanent fixture. Come on over and have a drink, pally."

I looked around. Why not? It was quiet.

"You just missed Dino," I said. "I think he left town today."

"I spoke to him. He's home, with Jeannie and the kids. And Sammy's there, right?"

"Yeah," I said, "right now he's probably on stage with Jerry Lewis."

"Yeah, I heard about that. And Joey's workin', so it's just you and me, pal."

"Where are you?"

"Where else? In the bar."

"Ten minutes, Frank," I said, and hung up.

\*\*\*

Del Webb bought the Sahara in 1961. He built a new skyscraper, which added four hundred rooms and brought the Sahara's number to a thousand. He also engineered a merger which included The Mint and the Lucky Strike Clubs. In '64 he accomplished a coup and brought the Beatles to Las Vegas.

I was surprised Frank was even discussing playing the Sahara with Webb. After all, he hated the Beatles. But then he had also hated Elvis when he came along, and that changed. He ended up having Elvis on his TV show when he came back from serving in Germany, and after that they got along great.

I went out to get in my Caddy and drive to the Sahara and then remembered that I had given the car to Big Jerry. I had one of the valets get me a cab.

"Caddy in the shop, Eddie?" he asked, as he held the door open for me.

"I loaned it out," I said, and closed the door before he could ask who to.

"Where to, Eddie?' the cab driver asked.

I knew most of the cabbies who worked the Sands on sight, and some by name. This one was Willy.

"The Sahara, Willy."

"Gotcha!"

We drove down the strip, brightly lit by all the neon marquees announcing the appearances of Red Skelton, Vic Damone, Steve & Eydie and, when we arrived at the Sahara, Louie Prima, Keely Smith and Buddy Hackett.

When Willy dropped me off, I tipped him big.

"Hey, thanks, Eddie. When ya headed back?"

"I don't know yet."

"I'll keep checkin'," he promised.

"Thanks, Willy."

When I got to the bar, Frank had managed to find some company.

"There's the man whose got Vegas wired," Buddy Hackett announced as I approached the table. "How ya doin', Eddie?"

"I'm doin great, Buddy," I said. "Aren't you supposed to be on stage?"

"Aw crap," Buddy said, "what time is it?" He looked at his watch. "Jesus, gotta go. See you guys later."

For a guy his size, Buddy moved quick and was gone.

"That guy's a riot," Frank said.

We shook hands and I sat down. A waiter came over quick.

"Two martinis, my good man, and step on it," Frank said.

"Yessir!"

"Martinis?" I said.

"Enjoy, pal. They're lettin' me drink for free."

"When did you get in, Frank?"

"This mornin'," he said. "I mighta passed Dino on the way. When I talked to him, he said he'd just got home. Jeannie was thrilled to see him. Did you hear Dino's kid's group hit the charts with a song? Jeez, none of them is even fourteen years old, yet."

"Dino, Desi and Billy—made up of Dean Paul Martin, Desi Arnaz Jr. and their friend, Billy Hinsche, had just hit #18 in the Billboard charts. Dean was very proud of his boy.

"I heard," I said.

"They might get more popular than me and Dino," Frank predicted.

His prediction fell a little short, though. They did hit #20 later that year with another song, but thereafter never made the top forty again. That was the way the business was.

"I heard tonight was Sammy and Jerry's second show," he said.

"That's right."

"You're not there."

"I saw it last night."

"How was it?"

"Bring back the Summit," I said.

"That bad?"

I winced.

"Let's just say I'm not a Jerry Lewis fan. I don't think Sammy needs him."

"Smokey doesn't need any of us," Frank pointed out. "The cat's got talent comin' out of his pores."

"Jack told me about the last few shows not drawing," I said.

"Oh, they were a draw," Frank said, "just not like they used to be. We could probably keep doin' them for a coupla more years, but it's time for us to move on. That's what Sammy's doin'. That's what I'd be doin' if I started playin' here."

"And Dean?"

"Dino can do whatever he wants," Frank said. "He's got movies, and his TV show, now. He's a busy cat."

"So are you."

"That's right. We're all busy. So don't cry for the Summit, Eddie."

"Maybe I just don't like change."

"Then you better get used to it," Frank said. "Vegas is changin'."

"Ain't it the truth."

"Howard Hughes is gonna take another run at it," Frank pointed out.

"Aw, geez . . ." I said.

"Yeah, you managed to stop him last time, but he's comin' back. That's what I hear."

"When?"

"Soon," Frank said. "Real soon."

The waiter came with our martinis and I raised my glass to Frank.

"Then I guess we better enjoy ourselves while we can," I said. "Here's to old Vegas."

"Amen," he said, and we clinked glasses. "Now tell me what you've been up to . . ."

## Chapter Fourteen

I sat and talked with Frank for a couple of hours, and then had to get back to the Sands. In those days I wasn't spending all that much time at home since my job took me out of the pits. Seemed like I was always in the casino or using a room in the hotel.

My conversation with Frank about old Vegas versus new Vegas had depressed me. The Rat Pack was splitting up, Howard Hughes was coming in, and the mob may have been on the way out. Things were going to change a lot if businessmen came in and took control. The mob may have been using the casinos to launder money, but they knew how to run things. I hated the idea of working for somebody other than Jack Entratter. Jack was Vegas from head to toe. Without him, things would go downhill in a hurry.

I caught a couple of hours shuteye in the hotel and was back on the casino floor early the next morning. I always took a turn before going into the Garden Café for breakfast, just to make sure nobody was going to interrupt my meal. It seemed the only time I ever had a meal outside the Café was when Frank or Dean called me to have dinner, and I met them somewhere else. Either that, or I had to wine and dine some high roller at the Golden Steer or the Bootlegger.

I looked around the Garden Café when I entered and didn't see Big Jerry. There was a good chance Danny was buying him breakfast at the Horseshoe on Fremont Street. I wondered how Danny's case was going, and if he had ended up using Gina as bait.

A pretty redheaded waitress named Terri took my order and poured me a cup of coffee. There were others I knew who were having breakfast there, but none that I cared to sit with. I was usually making sure somebody was having a good time, that on occasion it was nice to sit alone and not have to schmooze. Don't get me wrong, I loved Vegas and loved my job, but sometimes I couldn't hear myself think. Sometimes I'd like to just have dinner with a lady and wonder if I was going to get her into bed or not. That thought made me think of my lady high roller, Grace Kaufman. I wondered if she had waited for me in her suite last night. At least if she tried to pin me down, I could tell her I was with Frank Sinatra. That would impress her.

I was midway through my meal with Jack Entratter walked in. He looked around, spotted me, and stalked over.

"I heard from Grace Kaufman this morning," he said, sliding into the seat across the booth from me.

"Is that right?"

"She says you're not givin' her what she wants, Eddie," he said. "What does she want that's so hard to give her?"

I looked at him and said, "Sex."

"So? Send her somebody."

"No, Jack," I said, "she wants it from me."

He sat back, stared at me and said, "Oh."

"Yeah."

Terri came over and poured him a cup of coffee without asking.

"Thanks, doll," he said.

She smiled and flounced off.

"Killer freckles," he said.

"Yeah."

"Who is that?"

"Terri."

"They come and go so fast," he said, shaking his head. He sipped some coffee and set the cup down. "So, Eddie, would it be so bad? I mean, Grace Kaufman, she ain't bad lookin'."

"She's married, Jack."

"So? Come on, her husband's a hundred years old. He ain't gonna try to knock your block off for fuckin' his wife."

"I'm not worried about that," I said. "Besides, he could pay somebody to knock it off. But that's still not the point."

"Then what is?"

"I'm not a whore for hire," I said.

"Nobody said you were," Entratter said. "We're not sayin' she's gonna give you money. She just wants a little attention. It'd be you doin' your job."

"So it's you who'll be payin' me to be a whore," I pointed out.

"Stop sayin' whore!" he snapped, as Terri was walking by on her way to another table. She stopped and stared at him, and he just waved her on.

"Okay, look, I'm gonna leave it up to you because, yeah, it is your job to see to her needs," Entratter said. "Either fuck 'er or satisfy her some other way. Got it?"

"I got it."

"Good."

Terri went by again.

"It's too bad I don't fuck waitresses," he said, preparing to stand up. "Lemme know what happens."

"Yeah," I said, sourly, "okay."

He stopped short of standing and asked, "What have you been doin' that's so important you can't have sex with a beautiful woman?"

"I've been dealing with Sammy, Jerry Lewis, and seein' Frank."

"Frank's in town?" He frowned. "Where's he stayin'?"

"The Sahara," I said. "They're givin' him everything free."

"What the fuck?"

"Hey, you're the one who told me the Rat Pack's done here," I reminded him.

"That doesn't mean Frank has to turn traitor!"

"That's a little harsh, Jack."

He immediately adopted an expression I'd never seen on him before—shame.

"Yeah, yeah, I know," he said. "It's just that . . . things are changin', and you know I don't like change."

"Neither do I," I said, "but what can we do about it?"

"Nothin'!" he snapped. "That's why I'm so pissed."

He stood up.

"I'll talk to you later."

"Right."

He stalked out of the restaurant with a dark cloud over his head.

"Did he call me a whore?" Terri asked, appearing at my side.

"No, doll, not you. He thinks you're amazing."

"Really?" She smiled.

"He likes the freckles."

"Groovy," she said. "You want anything else, Eddie?"

"No, Terri, thanks. I'm just going to finish this."

"Okay."

Satisfied with what I'd told her, she flounced away, hips and butt twitching happily.

I finished my breakfast.

# Chapter Fifteen

Just before leaving the Garden Café, Terri brought a phone over to my booth and plugged it in.

"Call for you, Eddie."

"Yeah?" I said into the phone.

"Eddie, it's Sammy."

"What's up, Sam? How did last night go?"

"If you ask the audience, it went well," he said. "Jerry wasn't happy with it."

"What now?" I asked.

"He's got too much on his mind," Sammy said.

"Is he in pain over something?" I asked. "Because I'm not an analyst."

"Of course he's in pain," Sammy said. "Jerry believes that comedy comes from pain. But that's not it. It's something else. I have never known Jerry to be violent, but I think it's pent up in him, now. You gotta get through to him."

"Me?" I said. "You're his friend."

"It can't be done by a friend," Sammy said. "He won't talk to a friend."

So much for having Dean approach him.

"Eddie, you've got to make him talk to you."

"And how do I do that?"

"I don't know," he said. "Use that old Eddie G. charm of yours. Or does that only work on females?"

"From your lips to God's ears, Sam," I said, and we hung up.

***

I spent the afternoon as I usually did, but in the back of my mind I was trying to figure out how to use that "Old Eddie G. charm" on Jerry Lewis to get him talking.

When I got a break late in the afternoon I went to the lounge and had the bartender give me a phone. I decided to check on Danny and Big Jerry. When I dialed Danny's business number, his girl Penny answered. These days, she was his girl in more ways than one.

"Eddie! It's been too long since I've seen you," she complained.

"I feel the same way," I said. "Is Danny there?"

"No, he's out with the big guy."

"Are they workin' on that case he needed Gina for?" I asked.

"Gina, yeah," she said, not sounding happy. "She's the bait."

"Is she okay?"

"She's fine. Well enough to keep makin' passes at Danny."

"Penny, you have nothin' to worry about."

"Oh no?" she asked. "Have you seen her legs?"

"Yes, but I've also seen you, sweetie," I said.

"That's nice."

Penny was a great girl, and pretty, but she wasn't showgirl pretty, and she didn't have Gina's legs. But I didn't have the time to keep stroking her bruised ego.

"Is everything going according to Danny's plan?" I asked.

"Not yet, but he's hopeful."

"Is Jerry with Danny, or Gina?"

"He's with Danny, and they're watching Gina."

"Okay," I said, "if you hear from them, let 'em know I was just checking in."

"Will do. And Eddie?"

"Yeah."

"In the future, don't introduce Danny to any more showgirls."

"Gina's not—okay, yeah, you got a deal."

We hung up.

## Chapter Sixteen

I spent the early evening trying to find a high stakes poker game for one of my whales. The minimum buy-in he wanted was so high, it took me a while to find five other players willing to pony up that amount. Then I had to find a place for the game, and we ended up doing it in a room at the Riviera.

During those negotiations, I had three other things on my mind; what were Danny, Jerry and Gina involved in? How would I get Jerry Lewis to open up to me? And should I have sex with Grace Kaufman as part of my job?

The Grace Kaufman thing was dicey. If I did it as part of my job, I was a whore. If I did it because I was in a dry spell and she was attractive, that was okay. Although I knew the phone numbers of two or three other ladies who might be happy to help me break a dry spell. Two were showgirls and one was a dealer at the Flamingo.

The Danny/Jerry thing was odd, because I wasn't usually kept on the outside of something like that. All I knew was Danny needed a showgirl-type for bait, and asked Gina, and then needed Big Jerry to watch her. It sounded dangerous.

And then there was Jerry. How the hell was I supposed to get someone I didn't particularly like, who didn't seem to like me, to open up? Sammy seemed to have a lot of faith in me. But what if Sammy was wrong?

I had the feeling I needed to talk to someone who knew Jerry very well, and there only seemed to be one person for that.

\*\*\*

"Hi, Jeannie, it's Eddie Gianelli from Vegas," I said, when Jeannie Martin answered my call.

"Eddie, it's so nice to hear your voice," she exclaimed. "How are you?"

"I'm good. How are you and the kids?"

"We're great, but you didn't call to ask me that. You want Dean."

"I do."

"He's not here, Eddie."

"The golf course?"

"No, he's actually at the studio. They're blocking his show."

I knew "blocking" was a show biz term, not that I knew exactly what it meant.

"Is it important?" she asked.

"I don't know, Jeannie," I said. "How well do you know Jerry?"

"Jerry Lewis?" she asked. "Quite well. Back in the day we ate with Jerry and his wife all the time. Of course, recently we've fallen out of touch."

"I understand that," I said. "But . . . maybe you can answer a question for me."

"I'll try, Eddie."

"Have you ever witnessed Jerry being . . . violent?"

"Violent?" she asked. "I've seen him angry, frustrated, but do you mean . . . physically violent?"

"That's what I mean."

"Then the answer is no."

"Do you think he's capable of violence?"

"I think we're all capable of it, Eddie," she said. "But Jerry . . . there's deep-seeded pain there, Eddie, that Jerry keeps buried. It only comes out in his antics on stage."

"That's what I've heard," I said, "that his comedy comes from pain."

"Not only his," she said. "He believes all comedy comes from pain."

"So I've heard."

"But to answer your question definitively," she said, "I've never seen him be violent, but nothing would surprise me when it comes to Jerry Lewis."

"Okay," I said. "Thanks for talkin' to me."

"Do you want Dean to call you?"

"Is it hard for Dean to talk about Jerry?" I asked. "I don't want to cause him any . . . discomfort."

"I'll talk to him," Jeannie said. "Why don't we leave it up to him whether he calls you or not?"

"That's a good idea, Jeannie," I said. "Thanks again."

"Come to L.A. some time, Eddie," she said. "I'll make you a home-cooked meal."

"You've got a deal."

"And bring a girl."

"Um—"

"Or I'll fix you up," she said, and hung up.

Being fixed up by Jeannie Martin might not be a bad idea, since I had no idea what girl I'd take to dinner at Dean Martin's house.

But Dean was kind of a recluse. When he wasn't on stage, or on the golf course, he preferred to be home alone with his family.

It was the reason I had never expected to be invited to his house and was okay with it.

## Chapter Seventeen

I was still considering my options that afternoon when a face appeared in the casino, one I was never glad to see. I had just unraveled a smallish problem that had, at least, served to occupy my mind and distract me, when I saw Las Vegas Detective Hargrove coming across the casino floor towards me.

"Eddie, can we talk?" he asked.

"When have we ever been able to talk, Hargrove?"

"Yes, I understand your attitude," Hargrove said, "but we need to talk. Let's go somewhere."

"The bar," I said. "You want a drink?"

"I'll have a beer."

"Come on."

I led him to the lounge, where we sat at the bar. I asked the bartender for two beers, waited until we had them in hand.

"Thanks," Hargrove said, which shocked me.

"Thanks? What's goin' on, Hargrove?"

"I have a problem," he said.

"I have my own problems," I said. "Why come to me?"

"Because I can't trust anybody in my department," Hargrove said. "I need somebody on the outside, and someone who doesn't like me would probably be best."

"Well," I said, "that would be me."

"Exactly."

"What's the problem, Hargrove?" I didn't know that I intended to agree to help him, but I sure wanted to hear what his trouble was. It probably couldn't have happened to a nicer guy.

"I've been suspended," he said.

"Really?"

"Don't sound so happy about it," Hargrove said.

"Oh, sorry. Is this the first time this has ever happened to you?"

"Yes."

"What's it about?"

"I've been accused of taking bribes."

"And were you taking bribes?"

"No! I don't do that. I have a lot of faults, Eddie, but I don't take money."

He was so adamant, I believed him.

"So what is it you think I can do?" I asked.

"Clear me."

"Why me?"

"Like I said," he replied, "I need somebody who doesn't like me to clear my name."

"There must be a lot of people who fit the bill," I offered.

"I also need somebody who's competent enough to get it done."

"That's what you think of me?" I asked him. "I'm competent?"

"At the very least," Hargrove said.

"Hargrove," I said, "you've got a lot of nerve asking this of me. You hate me."

"That's true."

"And I hate you."

"Still true."

"So what makes you think I'll help you?"

"Because," he said, "if I get kicked off the force, you don't know who you'll draw to stay on your ass."

"Ah," I said, "you mean, the devil I know . . ."

"Yeah," Hargrove said. "Besides, you might be interested to know who's been accused of bribing me."

"Oh? Who?"

He paused, probably for dramatic effect.

"Your good buddy, Danny Bardini."

# Chapter Eighteen

"What are you talkin' about?" I asked. "Danny wouldn't do that." And, of course, I meant Danny wouldn't do that with Hargrove, because the dick would turn him in. But I did know that Danny had greased a lot of palms, in his day.

"Your friend knows I'd turn him in if he ever tried to bribe me."

"I would think everybody you work with knows you'd do that," I said. "Why don't your bosses?"

"Because I've got a new boss," he said, "and there's an Internal Affairs detective with a hard-on for me."

"Then it sounds like you've got a hard way to go, Hargrove," I said. "But I still don't see why I'd help you, even if Danny is involved."

"Look, your buddy is trying to bring down a hard man in this town," Hargrove said. "And it's somebody I've been after for years."

It sounded like he was talking about me, except for the "hard man" part. I was a sweetheart.

"So why haven't you ever thought to work together?"

"We had a conversation once about it," Hargrove admitted. "We decided our dislike for each other was too much. So what we agreed on was that we'd stay out of each other's way."

"When was this?" Danny had never told me about this conversation.

"Months ago."

"And?"

"Somebody took our photo together," Hargrove said, "and sent it to Internal Affairs. It sat there for a while until I got a new boss. My old boss would never have believed this about me, but the new guy is a hard-ass. So he put me under investigation and yanked my badge."

"And Danny?" I asked. "Is he after Danny?"

"I don't know," Hargrove said. "He might be. I think that's gonna be for you to find out."

I wondered if this was the same case Danny was working on, with Jerry and Gina? I decided not to ask Hargrove. I'd ask Danny.

"So whatayou say, Eddie?"

I stared at Hargrove. Did I want to save his ass so he could keep his badge and continue to hound me?

"I tell you what," I said. "I'll look into it, and if I have to do something to save Danny's ass, and it happens to save yours, too, so be it."

"I'm gonna accept that," Hargrove said. He reached into his jacket and took out a brown envelope, folded the long way so it would fit. "This is the file."

I took it. It felt light.

"The whole file?"

"The salient parts."

Salient? Was this the Detective Hargrove I knew?

"One more thing," he said.

"What's that?"

"Don't try to contact me," he said. "I'll check in with you from time to time and see what you've decided."

"Yeah, okay."

He drank half his beer and set it down.

"Thanks for the drink. I'll be in touch."

He stood up and left the lounge. I looked at the envelope in my hand and decided to wait until I was alone to open it. I refolded it and stuck into my jacket pocket.

It had become very evident that between Jerry Lewis, and whatever mess Danny had gotten himself—and maybe Jerry and Gina—in, I was going to need to be off the clock. Entratter never had a problem with that, as long as it involved somebody from the Rat Pack.

I'd just have to see if he felt the same about Jerry Lewis.

## Chapter Nineteen

I found Jack in his office, bypassing his girl's empty desk. She must've been on a break. He sat back in his chair as I walked up and sat down across from him.

"I need to be off the clock for a while."

"Why did I have the feeling you were gonna say that?" he asked. "It must be the look on your face."

"I'll have to work on that," I said.

"Okay, I'll bite," Entratter said. "Why do you need to be off the clock?"

"Well, one reason is Jerry Lewis."

"What's wrong with him?"

"That's what I'm going to find out."

"He asked for your help?"

"No," I said, "the request came from Sammy."

"Not Dino?"

"Now you know he and Jerry don't talk much since they broke up," I said. "No, it was Sammy."

Entratter nodded.

"Okay, so Sammy. What else?"

"Ah," I said, "Danny's gotten himself involved in something hinky, and now he's got Jerry Epstein involved, and Gina, from the Garden—"

"Gina the showgirl-in-waiting waitress?" he asked.

"That's her."

"What a set of legs."

"Which is why Danny wanted her," I said. "As bait."

"Bait? For what?"

"I have to find out," I said, "and I need the time to do it."

"Okay," he said, "Sammy and Danny. Anythin' else?"

"I think I may need your help."

"When? And with what?"

"Detective Hargrove came to see me."

"And you're not in jail?"

"He asked for my help."

"What?" Entratter looked like he was going to choke. "With what?"

"Well, he told me this story about getting suspended, said it involved taking bribe money from Danny—"

"Danny again?"

"Danny still," I said. "I don't know if the bribe happened on a separate case, or the one Danny's workin' now, with Jerry and Gina."

"Sounds like you've got a lot to find out."

"Yeah, I don't trust Hargrove," I said.

"You think he might be settin' you up for somethin'?" Jack asked.

"He might be."

"And you might need me to get you out, at some point?"

"Somethin' like that."

"What about your Kennedy contact?" he asked.

"I played that card once," I said. "I think it was a one-time Get-Out-of-Jail-Free card."

"Well," Jack said, "you've got my number, Eddie. You call and I'll come runnin'."

"Thanks, Jack."

"Just don't let Hargrove, or Bardini, get you killed," Entratter said. "I don't have anybody to replace you."

I stood up.

"That's because I'm Eddie G." I said, "you know, '*the* guy.'"

"That's you."

I turned to leave.

"Hey, if my girl is back from her break send her in, will ya?"

"Sure."

I went out the door and found her just settling in at her desk.

"Boss wants you," I said.

"Thanks," she said, and stood back up again. She was a pretty thing. All Jack's girls have been pretty, but they also had another thing in common.

They had a brain. He made sure of that.

"Can I use your phone while you're in there?" I called after her.

"You're Eddie G.," she said. "Can't you do anything you want?"

I didn't know what that comment meant, but I couldn't stop to figure it. I dialed Danny's home number, but there was no answer. I didn't try the office again. I didn't want to worry Penny. So I dialed Jerry's room. No answer, but I didn't expect one. I couldn't dial Gina because I didn't know her number.

I got out of there before Jack's girl got back.

\*\*\*

I couldn't just be off the clock. I had to let some people know, so they wouldn't be looking for me. For that I went down to the casino floor.

I let a few key people know about my situation—nothing specific, just that I was going to be away for a while. Then I headed for the front desk of the hotel to let them know, when one of the cigarette girls came sashaying over to me. Her name was Lila.

"Hey, Lila," I said. "What's up?"

"Somebody lookin' for you, Eddie," she said.

"Oh? Who?"

"Says he's Jerry Lewis," she said, "but he doesn't look like it, to me."

"Why not?"

"Well, he looks too serious," she said, "and he didn't call me laaaaadeeee." She raised her voice in a lousy Jerry Lewis impersonation. "I mean—" She leaned close to me and lowered her voice, "—he's supposed to be funny, right?"

"And?"

"Well, this man isn't very funny," she said. "In fact, he looks downright . . . depressed."

"Okay, Lila," I said, "I'll go and see who he is. Now all I need to know is . . . where is he?"

# Chapter Twenty

Jerry Lewis was sitting at a table in a corner of the Silver Queen Lounge. Patrons in the lounge were used to seeing celebrities, both up on stage and in the audience. Sometimes they're approached for autographs, but not as often as they used to be.

"Jerry," I said, sitting across from him. "Folks leavin' you alone?"

"They are now," he said, seriously.

I assumed that meant he had told somebody off in a way that the message was projected to everyone.

"What're you drinkin'?" I asked, looking at his red drink.

"Cranberry juice."

I turned and waved to the blonde waitress whose name was Cassie. Unlike Gina, she would always stay a waitress, because she didn't have the legs—or the height—for a showgirl. But she was cute enough to do very well on tips. She came over and I asked for a beer and another cranberry juice. "Sure, Eddie," she said, and gave Jerry a dirty look before walking off.

I looked at Jerry.

"She was getting too chatty," he explained.

"The waitresses do that."

Cassie brought the drinks, sniffed at Jerry and left us alone.

"Can we talk here?" he asked. "Doesn't somebody start performing soon?"

"Not for another hour or so," I said. "It should be pretty quiet until then."

The other patrons had already begun to turn away and ignore us.

"So, what's goin' on, Jerry?" I asked.

"What did Sammy tell you?" he asked.

"Not much," I said. "Just that he thought you might need help."

"From you?"

"From somebody," I said. "If the problem's connected to Vegas in some way then, yeah, from me."

Jerry stared at me for a few moments, so I took the opportunity to sip some beer.

"Sam must've told you more," he said, then.

"Well then, you're gonna have to ask Sam that," I said. "Right now I'm available to listen, if you want to talk."

"Okay," Jerry Lewis said, "but it can't go any further than this."

I tapped my finger and said, "No further than the top of this table."

"Frank says you're trustworthy."

"You talked to Frank about me?"

"He talked about you one night—oh, this was months ago. I never thought I'd have to find out for myself, though."

"Well, we're not gonna find out anything unless you talk to me," I said. "And the fact that we're here means you've made up your mind. Or has it?"

He played with his glass, turning it in circles, but not taking a drink. Finally, he pulled his hand away.

"Eddie," he said, "I need you to keep me from killing somebody."

I don't know if he expected that to shock me, but I just lifted my beer and drank.

"Did you hear me?" he asked.

"I'm sorry, Jerry," I said, "but I'm havin' a hard time believin' that you could—or would—kill anyone."

"Well then, you don't know me very well," he said.

"I realize that," I said, "and that's the problem. Suppose you tell me why you think you intend to kill somebody. And then we'll go from there."

# Chapter Twenty-One

"We all have things about us we don't want people to know," Jerry Lewis said.

"I think that's true."

"And that's why somebody invented blackmail."

"So somebody's blackmailin' you?"

"Let me tell it," he said.

"Okay, go ahead."

"My father's name is Danny Lewis. He is—or was—a nightclub entertainer. He worked vaudeville, and the Borscht Belt. Do you know what that is?"

"I'm from New York, Jerry," I said. "The Borscht Belt are the summer resort hotels in the Catskill Mountains, where entertainers like your father and lots of others plied their trade—mostly musicians and comedians."

"Right. My father's a singer and dancer. He's sixty-three now, but he's still doin' it. I did it for years with him and my mother. It's where I learned."

"Okay," I said, "we've established what the Borscht Belt is and what it means to your family. Where do we go from there?"

Abruptly, Jerry pushed away his glass of cranberry juice and said, "I need a real drink for this."

"What'll ya have?" I asked, like a bartender.

"Scotch."

I waved Cassie over and asked for a scotch. I didn't tell her it was for Jerry Lewis. She might've spit in it.

When she brought it over, I took it from her and set it down in front of him. He picked it up, sipped it, grimaced, then sipped again and put it down. I had no idea if this was his drink of choice, or his first time.

"Go ahead," I said.

"I'm gonna make this short," Lewis said. "I love my father, but he did something once—I'm not even sure what it was—that he doesn't want anybody to know about, so neither do I."

"And somebody knows about it?"

"Yes."

"And is threatening to go public."

"Yes."

"Do you know who?"

"No, I just know that whoever it is, he's from Vegas."

"So that's the real reason you're here," I said. "Not the act with Sammy."

"That came along, and gave me a reason to come," he said. "This sonofabitch wants me to meet him and pay him."

"And?"

"And I think if I meet with him," the comedian said, "I'll kill 'im."

He hurriedly lit a cigarette with shaky hands, blew the smoke out raggedly.

"Have you thought about going to the police? The F.B.I.?"

"Thought about it, rejected the idea."

"So you were plannin' on doin' this yourself."

"Yes," he said, "until Sammy started to ask questions. Then he introduced us."

"And you remembered what Frank said about me."

"Yeah, and Sammy says the same thing. You're the guy to trust."

"Have you told Sammy about this?"

"I ain't told anybody but you, Eddie," he said. "That's the way I want to keep it, for now." He reached across the table and closed his hand around my right wrist. "I need your word on this."

"Jerry," I said, "who would I tell and, more importantly, what would I tell 'em? I don't know anything."

"You know enough," Lewis said. "In fact, you know about what I know."

"Jerry, whoever this was who contacted you, what made you so sure he knows anythin'?"

"He's supposed to tell me, when we meet," Lewis said.

"So you still intend to meet with him?"

"I have to," he said. "What I need is for you to come along to guide me, since this is your town."

"And keep you from killing him."

He dragged on the cigarette, drank some scotch, and said, tightly, "Yes."

\*\*\*

I made Jerry Lewis take a break, put out his cigarette, got rid of the scotch and told Cassie to bring us a pot of coffee and two cups. I waited until we both had our cups full, and he had taken a few sips.

"Jerry, I need you to calm down," I said. "You're wound up so tight you're gonna explode."

"Don't worry," he said, "when I explode it's always on stage."

"So you're always wound this tight?"

"Let's just say the phrase 'laid back' ain't in my vocabulary."

"Maybe you need therapy."

"I went to a psychiatrist once," he said. "Do you know what he told me?"

"What?"

"That he could work with me to negate the pain I feel from my childhood, but if we were successful, I might not be funny, anymore."

"So you have to feel pain in order to be funny?"

"On stage, yes," Lewis said. "I'm not prepared to give that up. So like I said, when I explode, it's on stage . . . or on camera."

"All right," I said, "tell me you talked to your father about this."

"I did."

"Did the blackmailer contact him?"

"No, the only contact has been with me."

"Why do you think that was?"

He shrugged.

"I have the money."

"When you talked to your father, did he tell you what it was he did that he doesn't want anyone to know about?"

I saw a muscle jump in Lewis' jaw, and then he said, "No."

"But he told you it was bad."

"He told me no one should ever find out," he answered, "especially my mother."

"I see," I said, though I didn't see much. "So your mother knows nothing about this situation?"

"Not a thing, and I want to keep it that way."

"Fine with me."

"Eddie . . . can you agree to help me, and keep quiet about it?"

I stared at him. Did I want to get involved and, if not, how could I tell Sammy? Up to now I'd never turned down any of the guys, whether they were asking me to help them, Marilyn, Ava or Judy.

But Jerry Lewis?

## Chapter Twenty-Two

Jerry Lewis' blackmailer had not contacted him since he arrived in Vegas. I told him to let me know when he did, and we'd go from there.

"I've got to go upstairs and work on tonight's act," he said. He stood, but didn't leave, just stared at me for a moment. "This wasn't easy for me to talk about, Eddie."

"Jerry," I said, "we really didn't talk about much. Think about it, and let's see if there's anythin' else you can tell me next time we meet."

"I don't even know much more myself," he said, and walked out.

Did I believe him? It just seemed to me he was holding back. I don't usually like to get involved in something if I don't know the whole story.

Which reminded me . . .

I waved to Cassie and asked her to bring me a phone. She carried it over, plugged it in and set it down on the table.

"That was a big disappointment," she said, before leaving.

"Jerry Lewis?" I said. "Cassie, I think you'll find it disappointing to meet most of your idols."

"Thank God he wasn't one of my idols," she said. "I've met Frank Sinatra and Dean Martin in here, and they're wonderful!"

"Yeah, they are," I said. "Stick to the crooners and leave the comedians alone, that's my advice."

"I think I'll do that, Eddie. Thanks."

As she walked away, I lifted the receiver and dialed Danny's office number. Once again, I got Penny, and this time I was kind of insistent.

"I really need to talk to 'im, Penny," I said. "Detective Hargrove came to me with a story I need to check out."

"I'll tell him, Eddie," she promised. "You should hear from him sometime today."

"I hope so."

We hung up and I sat there a moment with my hand on the phone. What else did I have to do? I'd gotten myself taken off the clock, as far as Jack Entratter was concerned, to help Jerry Lewis. So what did it matter if I also helped Danny? And by doing that, probably helping Jerry and Gina, as well.

But now I was in a position where I was waiting for phone calls, one from Jerry Lewis, the other from Danny.

It was now a matter of, what do I do now?

Off the clock or not, I decided to walk around the casino and see if I was needed for anything.

## That Old Dead Magic

There was always something to be done, decisions to make, on the casino floor:

Red Skelton wanted his credit limit increased. I okayed it.

A hot shooter at the craps table wanted the table limit raised. It wasn't really my call, Entratter wasn't around, and neither was a pit boss, so I said yes. Nobody would bitch.

A heavy blackjack loser wanted a free dinner. Why not?

A heavy roulette winner wanted a free dinner. Definitely.

Jack Jones was singing in the lounge. I listened for a bit. He was no Vic Damone, but he was okay.

I had it in my mind to take the night off and go see Steve and Eydie at the Riviera. In the end, I decided to stay put. But when the show started in the Copa Room with Jerry Lewis and Sammy Davis, I made sure I wasn't there.

Entratter came down late, after closing his office, and spotted me on the casino floor.

"I thought you were off."

"So did I," I answered. "I'm waitin' for a call."

"Are you the one who upped Skelton's limit?" he asked.

"Yeah. Problem?"

"No," he said, "no problem . . . just don't do it again."

"Right."

"How's it goin' with Jerry Lewis?"

"It's goin'," I said. "We'll probably be doin' something tomorrow."

"Make sure he stays happy."

I didn't bother telling him that the Jerry Lewis I had met was never happy.

"And let me know when you're back to work."

"I was around all day, Jack," I said, "even handling some things I shouldn't be handling."

"Oh . . . well, thanks for that. I'm sure I'll hear about it, later."

"I'll do my best with Jerry," I promised.

He started away, then turned back.

"Did he say anythin' to you about him and Dino?" he asked.

"No, not a thing."

"I still wonder what that was all about," Entratter said. "What a pair they were."

"They both seemed to have done okay for themselves since the split," I commented.

"Yeah," Entratter said, "yeah, you're right about that. See ya later, Eddie."

He left the casino floor.

## Chapter Twenty-Three

When Danny called, I wasn't near a phone. He left a message for me at the front desk of the hotel. One of the desk clerks handed it to me. It said: DINNER, THE HORSEHOE 7 P.M. I checked my watch. It was six-fifteen. I was halfway to the parking lot when I remembered Big Jerry had my caddy. I reversed my direction, went out front and had one of the valets get me a cab.

Whenever Danny wanted to meet me at the Horseshoe, he didn't mean the steakhouse, he meant the coffee shop in the basement. I took the long escalator ride down and saw both Danny and Jerry seated in a booth, waiting.

"Just got your message," I said, joining them.

"That's fine," Danny said. "You're not late. We waited to order."

A waitress came over and took our orders—burger platters for all of us.

"You're eatin' French fries?" I asked Jerry.

"I won't eat 'em all, damn it," he swore.

"What's goin' on, Eddie?" Danny asked.

"Where's Gina? Is she okay?"

"At the moment she's home, in her apartment," Danny said. "We're gonna be pickin' her up later tonight. Is that what you needed to talk to me about? You're worried about Gina?"

"Gina's a good kid," Jerry said. "We ain't gonna let nothin' happen to her. She's just gonna—"

"Hey, Jerry," Danny said. "Pipe down."

I looked at Danny. I couldn't remember the last time he wanted to keep something from me.

"It's just a case I can't talk about," Danny said, as he noticed my stare. "Why don't you tell me what's on your mind? Penny said somethin' about Hargrove?"

"Yeah, he came to see me," I said. "He says he's been suspended and needs my help."

"What?" Danny was aghast. "That asshole is always tryin' to put you away. Why would you help him?"

"He says he was suspended because he's suspected of takin' bribes . . ."

"So?"

". . . from you."

"What?"

"Jesus," Jerry said to Danny, "you bribed a cop? I didn't think you had it in ya.'

"I don't!" Danny said. "I mean, I never did." He looked at me. "It's not true."

"Well," I said, "I'm thinkin' maybe Hargrove is trying to set us up for somethin'."

"That makes more sense," Danny agreed.

"I don't know if he's really been suspended."

"Well," Danny sad, "I'd offer to find out, but I'm workin' this case pretty heavy."

"Then I'll try to find out," I said. "Maybe I'll let him think I'm tryin' to help him, when I'm actually tryin' to help us."

"Sounds good," Danny said. "Jesus, I'd love to kick his ass old school style, but then I'd end up in the can."

"Maybe when this is all over," Jerry said, "I could—"

"No, Jerry!" I snapped.

"He'd never know it was me," Jerry said. "I've done it a million times before. I'll just put him in the hospital."

Danny and I exchanged a glance, and then we both said, "No," at the same time.

"Think about it," Jerry said.

The waitress came with our orders then, and set them down on the table. Danny and I drank coffee, and Jerry just had a big glass of ice water.

While we ate, I told them both that Jerry Lewis had a problem I was trying to help him with it.

"Aw hell," Danny said, "you're just tryin' to get me back for not tellin' you about my case."

"I'm not that shallow, Danny," I told him. "Lewis doesn't want to talk to anyone about it."

"What's he like?" Jerry asked. "I mean, he's funny, right?"

"Not at all," I said.

"You're kiddin', right?" Danny asked.

"I kid you not," I said. "The guy's one of the most serious people I've ever met. He's angry, and in pain, and the only place he gets a release is when he's performing."

"That's crazy," Danny said.

"Yeah, it is," I said. I told them what Jerry Lewis said his analyst told him.

"Wait a minute," Jerry said. "So the guy's gotta stay in pain to be funny?"

"That's what he believes," I said.

"Now that *is* crazy," Jerry said, picking up a French fry.

"That's true of all comics, is it?" Danny asked. "Buddy Hackett's my favorite. I don't want that to be true of him."

"You'd have to ask him," I said. "All I know is what I heard from Lewis."

"Rickles," Jerry said. "It can't be true of Don Rickles. The guy's hilarious."

We all picked up our burgers and bit into them. As usual, the Horseshoe coffee shop burgers were perfect. But that's about all that was.

## Chapter Twenty-Four

We finished eating and got refills on the coffee and water.

As the waitress took the plates away, Jerry looked like he was going to cry over the fries he left behind.

"What's botherin' you, Eddie?" Danny asked.

"I gotta admit," I said, "You and Jerry and Gina are workin' on somethin' together and I'm feelin' a little left out."

"Eddie," Danny said, "buddy, don't be that way. You're a busy guy, and I really didn't need you for this one. Jerry's doin' the job."

"Fine," I said, "you're right, I am busy. I've got to handle Jerry Lewis because Sammy Davis asked me to, and I've gotta watch out for Hargrove, who's probably tryin' to pull somethin'."

"And if he's tryin' somethin' that'll hurt us both," Danny said, "lemme know. I'll make time."

"And if you decide you want his ass kicked—" Jerry started.

"I got it, Jerry!" I said. "You'll put him in the hospital."

I stood up.

"I'm heading back to the Sands."

"We have some things to talk about," Danny said, "so Jerry and I will be here a little while longer."

Jerry looked up at me and said, "Dessert."

I left them to it.

\*\*\*

Heading back to the Sands, I was wondering how to confirm that Hargrove was or wasn't suspended, without actually talking to him. I wondered if a black lifer named Everett was still his partner, or if he had yet another new one?

When I got to the Sands, I went to the house phones and called Hargrove's office. When a cop answered, though, I asked for Detective Everett.

"Everett," he said into the phone.

"Detective Everett, this is Eddie Gianelli, from the Sands Hotel and Casino."

"Eddie G.," he said. "Yeah, I remember you from that whole Miami/Jackie Gleason thing a few months back."

"Right," I said. "At the time you were Detective Hargrove's partner. Is that still the case?"

He made a rude sound with his mouth and asked, "Whatayou think? I got out of that partnership as soon as I could. Why?"

"Hargrove came by to see me, claims he's been suspended for suspicion of takin' bribes."

Silence.

"Would you know anythin' about that?" I asked.

He didn't answer right away.

"Everett?"

"I'm only gonna say this because I don't like Hargrove," he finally said. "Don't believe anythin' he tells you. Get it?"

"I get it," I said. "Thanks."

"And don't call me again."

We hung up.

I sat there a few moments, wondering how Hargrove thought he'd get away with that story? And what did he want me to do? Stick my nose where it didn't belong so he could cut it off? He'd already tried that numerous times. What was his game?

As I was crossing the lobby, Cassie from the Garden Café, came running over to me.

"Eddie!"

"Easy, Cassie. What's wrong?"

"Nothing's wrong," she said. "In fact, everything's right, except that I can't find Gina. Do you know where she's been?"

"As far as I know she got a job on the side."

"But . . . waitressing is her job on the side," Cassie said. "You know she's been waiting for a spot to open on somebody's line."

"Yeah, I know that."

"Well, the Riv's been trying to get ahold of her. They've got an opening, but if they can't find 'er they'll give it to somebody else."

"Okay," I said, "I don't know exactly where she is, but I'll get the message to her."

"Thanks Eddie," Cassie said. "She'll be crushed if she doesn't get this."

"Are you going to work?" I asked, since she was wearing street clothes and no apron.

"No, I'm on my way home," she said. "I just wanted to find you and tell you about the Riv. I'll be taking a breakfast shift tomorrow."

"I'll see you then," I said. "Goodnight."

"Goodnight, Eddie."

I watched her walk across the lobby and out the front door, then went into the casino. I had just seen Danny and Jerry. I wondered if I'd be able to get Danny on the phone if and when he went home. And that reminded me that one, I didn't know where Jerry was sleeping and two—and most important—I didn't know where my Caddy was.

## Chapter Twenty-Five

The next morning, I got a call at home, waking me from a deep sleep hours before I was planning to get out of bed. It was actually the first night I had spent in my own bed, in my little house, in a while.

"What?" I barked.

"What did you do to Jerry?" Sammy asked. He sounded as if he was in a panic.

"What're you talkin' about?"

"He was terrible last night," Sammy said. "His timing was all off. I had to sing three extra songs just to cover. What did you do to him?"

"I didn't do anything," I said. "We talked, he told me what's been botherin' him—"

"What is it?"

"That's for him to tell you, Sammy," I said, "not me. He swore me to secrecy."

"Aw, come on, man!" Sammy said. "I'm the one who brought you in on this."

"Right," I said, "to help Jerry Lewis. If he wants you to know more, Sammy, he'll tell you."

"Well, look," Sammy said, "see if you can get this over with fairly soon. When I'm on stage with him, I need him at his best."

"I'll see what I can do, Sam," I promised.

He hung up.

I went back to sleep.

\*\*\*

The phone rang again, waking me up a half hour later.

"What?" I barked.

"Don't bark at me, Eddie," Jack Entratter said.

"Oh, hey, Jack," I said. "What can I do for you?"

"Did I wake you from your beauty sleep?" Jack asked. "When you said you needed to be off the clock, I didn't think it was to get some sleep."

"I was up 'til late last night, trying to figure out my next move."

"Next move?"

"To help Jerry Lewis."

"And what does he need help with, exactly?" he asked.

"I can't say, Jack."

"Can't? Or won't?" Before I could answer he said quickly, "Never mind, never mind. I was calling about Mrs. Kaufman. She's been wonderin' where you are."

"Did you tell her that I'm busy?"

"Yes," he said, "I used your phrase and told her you were off the clock for a while."

"What did she say?"

"She said maybe the Sahara or the Riviera might be able to give her what she wants."

"Aw shit," I said.

"Yeah."

"She's talkin' about sex."

"I gathered that."

"Jesus, Jack," I said, "why don't you toss her a valet? Or a pool boy?"

"Not exactly her speed, I also gathered."

"What do you want from me?"

"I just thought I'd ask, Eddie," he said. "Thought maybe you might've changed your mind?"

"About bein' a whore?"

"Why do you have to keep usin' that word."

"What other word would you use?"

"Yeah, okay," he said. "Never mind. I'll figure somethin' out."

"What about you, Jack?" I asked.

"I think," he said, wryly, "if she wanted an old man, she'd fuck her husband."

He hung up.

***

The third time the phone rang I knew I was up for good.

"What?"

"Mr. G?" Jerry said.

"Jerry? You okay? You don't sound so good."

"Um, I think I need for you to see somethin'."

"What is it?"

"I'll give ya an address. Can you get over here right away?"

"Jerry, are ya okay?"

"I'm fine."

"And Gina?"

"Actually, she'll be here," Jerry said.

"Well, that's good," I said. "I've got a message for her."

"Good. Then this'll work for both of us," Jerry said. "Can you come?"

"I need a shower," I said, "and then I'll get a cab and be there. Just let me have the address."

He did, and then before he hung up he said, "I think you better prepare yourself, Mr. G."

"You're bein' very ominous, Jerry."

"If that means what I think it means . . . yeah."

He hung up.

## Chapter Twenty-Six

I showered and called a cab to take me to the address Jerry had given me. It was a residential neighborhood in nearby Henderson, which was located between Boulder City and Las Vegas.

I rang the doorbell and Jerry answered the door. I was shocked. He had turned in his ever present houndstooth jacket for jeans and a plaid polo shirt. I was further surprised to see loafers on his big feet. The get-up must've been for whatever part he was playing for Danny.

"Mr. G. Come on in."

I followed him into the living room, where Gina was sitting on a sofa. She stood as we entered. She was dressed cheaply, in a tight sweater, pedal pushers and heels that showed off her figure and long legs.

"Hello, Eddie."

"Gina," I said. "You're lookin' . . . different."

"It's the part I'm playing," she said.

"I've got a message for you," I said, "from Cassie. She says the Riviera's been callin' you. There's an opening on their line."

"Omigod!" she said, covering the bottom part of her face with her hands. "That's what I've been waiting for."

"I know it," I said, "and they won't hold it forever."

She dropped her hands, looking dismayed.

"I can't just walk out on Danny, Eddie," she said.

"You'll have to make up your own mind about that, Gina," I said. "Figure out what's more important to you." I turned to Jerry. "What did you want to show me?"

"It's out back," he said.

Gina sat back down, deep in thought, as Jerry and I left the room and walked through the house to the kitchen door in the back.

"Don't get too upset," Jerry said, with his hand on the doorknob.

"Upset about what?"

He opened the door and we stepped out. Behind the house was a garage, the door of which was open. Inside was my Caddy.

Or what was left of my Caddy.

"What the—"

I walked into the garage to get a better look. The outside of the car was charred, as if it had been on fire. The inside looked as if someone had taken a knife to the upholstery.

"What was the purpose of this?" I asked.

"Danny thinks it was revenge."

"For what?"

"Stickin' our noses where they don't belong."

"And have they approached Gina, yet? Your bait?" I asked.

"No."

"And do you have her staked out here?"

"Yes."

"Alone?"

"No, I'm with her."

"As what . . . husband? Boyfriend?"

"Her brother."

"Ah. And because you're in their way, they decided to burn your—my—car."

"That's what I believe," Jerry said.

"Where did it happen?"

"On the street," Jerry said. "I caught it and got the police department there before the car was a . . . total loss." He held up one hand, which had a bandage on it. "Burnt my hand tryin' to put it out."

"Bad?"

"Not too bad."

"Thanks for tryin' to save it, but don't do that again, okay? It's a car."

"But it's your Cadillac."

"Yeah, well," I patted his shoulder, "your safety—and Gina's—comes first."

But he looked at the Caddy as if he was going to cry.

"You've got insurance, right?" he asked.

"I've got plenty of insurance," I assured him.

"Good."

We went back into the house, found Gina still seated on the sofa.

"Sorry about your car, Eddie," she said.

"Neither one of you has to be sorry," I said. "I'm holdin' Danny responsible."

"But Danny wasn't even there," Gina said.

"If it wasn't for Danny, my car wouldn't have been there—wherever there was."

I turned to Jerry.

"What are you usin' for transportation now?"

"Danny got me another car," Jerry said. "A two-door sedan—a Dodge, I think."

"Good old American car," I said.

"Jerry, I'm going to have someone come out and look at the car and assess the damage, probably tow it."

"Okay, but don't come alone," Jerry said, "and don't send nobody, you know, official."

"You mean in uniform."

"Yeah, right."

"Okay, so maybe I'll wait until you're finished with this job for Danny before I call."

"No," Jerry said. "We're supposed to be acting normal. If I don't have an insurance guy come out and look, that'd be suspicious."

"Okay," I said. "I'll get somebody out here. But . . . if the house is being watched, don't you think it was dangerous to have me come out here at all?"

"Again," Jerry said, "We gotta look normal. You could be an insurance guy I brought around to look at it."

"Yeah, okay," I said. "This looks fresh." I could also smell the fire. "When did it happen.?

"Yesterday."

"Does Danny know?"

"He knows."

"Eddie," Gina said, "do you think I could go over to the Riv—"

"I think you'll have to talk to Danny about that, Gina," I said, cutting her off before she got her hopes too high.

"You could call," Jerry suggested.

"Yeah, I could do that," she said. "I'll get ahold of Cassie and find out exactly who to call. I'll use the phone in the kitchen." She looked at me. "Will you be here when I come back?"

"No. Danny probably doesn't want me here, at all."

As Gina went into the kitchen Jerry said, "I told him I was gonna call you, that you should know about the car right away."

"Thanks, Jerry," I said. "I appreciate that."

"I'm really sorry, Mr. G."

"Forget it, Jerry. Give me a call if you need anything."

"Will do."

We went to the front door and he let me out, locking it behind me.

# Chapter Twenty-Seven

I walked to the corner, then had to walk a few more blocks before I came to a section with businesses. There I was finally able to flag a cab down.

As I got out of the cab in front of the Sands, one of the valets yelled, "Where's the Caddy, Eddie?" but I pretended not to hear him. I was more upset about the condition of my car than I had let on to Jerry—or than I even knew myself.

I went straight to the front desk to check for messages. There were none. From there I went to the bar in the lounge and told the bartender, "Bourbon."

"Bad day, Eddie?" he asked, setting it down in front of me.

"You don't know the half of it," I said. "I'll follow this up with a beer, please."

"Comin' up."

I sipped my bourbon and thought about my second Caddy. The first one had been destroyed some time back, also when Jerry was around. Not his fault, though. And neither was this time. From what I'd seen of the car, it was probably salvageable, but that was going to depend on the insurance company. Without them, I'd have to foot the bill myself—which I would do, gladly. I had a mechanic who kept the car in tip-top shape for me. If anyone was going to cry about this situation, it was him.

The bartender brought me my beer, so I finished the bourbon and let him take the glass.

Whatever Gina was helping Danny with, it was probably going to cost her the spot on the Riviera line. That is, unless she called and made other arrangements. They certainly wouldn't be able to hold the spot for her indefinitely. Poor kid . . .

With no word from Jerry Lewis, I decided to work on the problem of Detective Hargrove. He had lied to me about being investigated, trying to get me to agree to help him. If I had agreed, what would have happened then? What information would he had given me—wait. He gave me a file. It was in my locker in the hotel's locker room.

I finished my beer, left the lounge to go and get it.

\*\*\*

Once I had the file in my hand I needed someplace to sit down and read it. The Sands had a back room that was sometimes used for high stakes poker games. At the moment, there was no game. I walked through the casino and into that back room closing the door behind me. There was one large, round poker table there. I sat in one of the comfortable chairs—we want all our players to be

119

comfy—put the folder on the green felt table top, but didn't open it. Not right away.

What if Hargrove was telling the truth? Okay, his ex-partner told me not to believe anything he said, but what if, this time, he was telling me the truth? What if in the folder was proof that Danny had bribed Hargrove. No, the detective wouldn't have given me proof that he took a bribe. But he might give me proof that Danny was paying bribes. What he didn't know was if that was the case, I wouldn't care. Danny Bardini did what he had to do to get his work done. If a cop was willing to take a buck to help, then why not pay it? One man's bribe was another man's operating expense.

But there had to be something in his file Hargrove wanted me to see, otherwise why give it to me? I looked down and opened it.

I flipped through the contents. There were typewritten reports, and follow-up reports. At the bottom of each report was Detective Hargrove's signature. Also, further along, the signature of a superior officer. In most cases, the superior officer's name was the same. So I already had something I didn't have before.

I settled my elbows on the table top, flipped back to the beginning of the file, and started to read.

# Chapter Twenty-Eight

According to the original report, Hargrove was investigating a man named Leo McKern, suspected of sex trafficking. Three young women had gone missing, and the police suspected McKern of being behind it. The follow-up reports indicated that Hargrove had isolated several of McKern's associates, and was intending to question them. However, when he went to talk to them, he found two dead and one missing.

A subsequent follow-up report indicated that the missing man—John Langston—was also an associate of private detective Danny Bardini.

In the final report, Hargrove suggested that Danny may have aided Langston in escaping from the police, and from Leo McKern.

I closed the folder. There was nothing in it to indicate that Danny had bribed, or tried to bribe, anyone, least of all Hargrove. But Danny's name did appear in the reports.

I needed to talk to Danny again, and this time he had to tell me exactly what he was working on, and if it involved Langston and McKern.

\*\*\*

"Eddie," Penny said, "I don't think Danny can drop what he's doing—"

"He told me to call if I need him, Penny," I said. "And I need him."

"I don't know where he is, at the moment," she said. "And to tell you the truth, I'm worried."

"What about Jerry?" I asked. "Is he at that house with Gina?"

"You know about that?"

"Jerry called me about my car."

"Oh, Eddie," she said, "I'm so sorry about your Caddy."

"It's just a car, Penny."

"Yes, but you love that car."

"Never mind that," I said. "Please check with Jerry to see if he knows where Danny is. I don't know where I'll be, but you can leave a message for me at the hotel desk at the Sands."

"Okay, Eddie," she said. "I'll try."

"Thanks, doll."

I had made the call from the bar in the lounge, so I hung up and pushed the phone back toward the bartender.

"Thanks."

"Any time, Eddie."

What was next? What was there for me to do while I waited to hear from Danny? And what if Jerry Lewis heard from his blackmailer and called me? Then what? Lewis or Danny?

There wasn't an act due on stage in the lounge for a couple of hours, so I walked to a corner table, waved the waitress away and opened the file folder again. Something was niggling at the back of my brain, and I found it in one of the follow-up files.

Kaminsky.

***

Kaminsky was a lawyer I used from time to time, when the Sands lawyers wouldn't do the trick. That's because he was a criminal lawyer.

"I had spotted his name in the file, only it hadn't registered at the time. In going back over it, I realized that he was Leo McKern's lawyer.

Once again, I used a cab to take me downtown to Kaminsky's office building. According to the directory in the lobby, he had moved to another floor. When I got there, I saw why. He apparently needed a bigger office.

I had called ahead and made an appointment, so I gave my name to his receptionist. It was odd, because he'd never had one of those before.

"Eddie Gianelli for Kaminsky."

"Ah, Mr. Gianelli," she said. "Mr. Kaminsky is expecting you. Go right in."

When I entered his office, Aaron Kaminsky, all five-feet-four of him, was seated behind a desk that was twice the size of his old one.

"Eddie G., my boy," he said. He talked like that, even though he was only a few years older than I was. He came around from behind the desk and shook my hand. "Good to see you. Have a seat."

He went back to his huge chair, and I sat across from him.

"What can I do for you, Eddie? You're not in trouble, are you?"

"Not the kind you mean," I said. "Not yet, anyway."

"Then what's up?"

"You have a client named Leo McKern."

He didn't react, then said, "Do I?"

"You do."

"And?"

"Do you know where he is?"

"If I have a client by that name," Kaminsky said, "I might or might not know where he is. What does it matter to you?"

"Hargrove came to me," I said, and explained the conversation we'd had. "Do you know if he was telling me the truth? Has he been suspended?"

"Not that I know of," Kaminsky said, then, "but what made you think I would know?"

"He's investigating your man, McKern," I said.

"I haven't said that this McKern is a client," Kaminsky told me.

"I get it, I get it," I said. "But I need to know if Hargrove is trying to set me up for something. Why tell me he's been suspended if he hasn't? What would he expect me to do about it?"

"Maybe you should ask him."

"I don't want him to know that I don't believe him," I said. "Not yet, anyway."

"I don't know what you want me to do, Eddie," Kaminsky said.

"Give me a sign, Kaminsky," I said. "You know, a nod, a wink? Is Hargrove just flat out playin' me?"

"Well," he said, "generally speaking, yes, he lies. Anybody who's ever dealt with him knows that. But sometimes it's to get his job done."

"And other times?"

"Other times he's just bein' a dick."

"And do you think this is one of those times?"

"I can't say, Eddie," Kaminsky said, "but I think it's a safe bet that the man just can't help himself."

I tried to think of some other questions to ask that didn't involve Leo McKern, since Aaron Kaminsky wouldn't talk about a client.

"Hey," I said, getting a sudden idea, "how about I give you a dollar, which makes me a client of yours? Could you talk to me then?"

"You'd be a client, that's true," Kaminsky said, "but I still can't talk about other clients."

"Okay, I get it," I said. "I was just lookin' for something I could use, something that would tell me what my next step should be."

Kaminsky studied me for a few moments, then sat back in his chair and sighed.

"Okay, look," he said, "I think your best bet is to act as if Hargrove lied through his teeth. Try not to do anything that he may have wanted you to do."

"That's . . . helpful, I guess," I said. Actually, it wasn't, but it went along with my own thoughts about how to proceed.

"Okay," I said, standing up, "thanks for talking to me."

Kaminsky stood and walked with me to the door of his office. When we got there, he put his arm around my shoulder.

"Listen," he said. "If you do find something out about this case Hargrove's working on—"

"You mean concerning Leo McKern?"

"I'm just saying," Kaminsky said, "I could use a heads up."

"Likewise," I said. "If you find out something you think you can share . . ."

"I'll give you a call." He patted me on the back.

As I walked past the receptionist, she smiled up at me prettily.

"Aaron said you'd be able to give me an address on Leo McKern," I lied.

"He couldn't have done that," she said, "since I don't know any Leo McKern."

"But you work here."

"I'm a receptionist," she said, "not a secretary. I don't know about his individual cases. I just answer the phone and make appointments. And, occasionally, I meet handsome friends of his."

"Friends?"

"That's what he told me," she said. "You're a friend, not a client."

"What's your name?"

"Camille," she said.

"Thank you, Camille."

"Uh, look," she said, "I can't help you with this McKern fella, but call me here if I can help in any . . . other way?"

# Chapter Twenty-Nine

I spent the rest of the day at the Sands, working off the books, and then settled in at the Garden Café for dinner. Following that, my intention was to go home. I could wait there for the phone to ring. But then something better than the phone ringing happened.

Big Jerry walked in.

He looked around, spotted me, and hurried over. He slid into the booth so hard that the whole thing moved.

"We got trouble, Mr. G."

"Trouble?" I asked "What trouble. This afternoon you seemed to have everything under control."

"That was before Gina called the Riviera about her spot," Jerry said,

"What happened?"

He snagged a fry from my plate.

"They told her she had to come down now, or no chance she'd have a spot."

"And?"

"And she went, and she didn't come back."

"You let her go alone?"

He fidgeted.

"She insisted, Mr. G. We argued. She said she'd be back in two hours. I said I just couldn't let her go. Then, to tell you the truth, she snuck out. That was about six hours ago."

"Did she get there?" he asked.

"I don't know, Mr. G., I didn't know who to call to find out."

"Well, I do."

I looked around, spotted Cassie and waved her over to ask for a phone. Once she brought it, I called the Riv and asked for the showgirl's house mother. There was one in every casino hotel.

I had a short conversation, then hung up and looked at Jerry.

"She never showed up," I said.

"Oh, no," Jerry said. "Shitshitshit . . . shit! The dick is gonna kill me."

"Maybe she blew the audition, and she's off somewhere, sulking," I offered.

"You know Gina, Mr. G.," Jerry said. "She wouldn't do that. She's a positive person."

Jerry and Gina must have done a lot of talking over the past few days of pretending to be a couple.

"Okay," I said, "think about this. How do you suppose she was gonna get to the Riv?"

"By cab?"

"So we have to check with the cab companies, and see who picked her up. Unless you have some idea which one she called."

"The Lake Mead Cab Company."

"What makes you say that?"

"There was a phone book on the table by the phone, and Lake Mead was circled."

"Did she circle it? Or was that phone book already in the house?"

"I don't know . . ."

"Okay," I said, "then that's where we'll start."

"We?"

"You want to go to Danny with this, right now? Let him know she got away from you?"

"Hell, no," Jerry said. "I wanna find her!"

"I know where the Lake Mead garage is," I said. "You got your car with you?"

"Yeah, out back."

"Let's do it, then."

"Will they still be open?"

"This is Vegas, fella," I said. "Everybody's open."

## Chapter Thirty

The garage of the Lake Mead Cab Company was on Paradise Road. Jerry pulled his sedan to a stop right in front. The garage doors were closed, but there was a light in the office. We got out, walked to the door and knocked.

"You gotta call for a cab, pal," a voice said from inside. "We're closed here."

"We don't want a cab," I called back. "We need to talk to you."

"About what?"

"A missing person."

The door opened a crack and a man with two five o'clock shadows on his face peered out.

"You more cops?"

"No," I said, "I'm Eddie Gianelli, from the Sands. We're lookin' for a missing girl that one of your drivers may have picked up."

The man opened the door wider and said, "Yeah, I heard-a you. Come on in."

We went inside and he closed and locked the door. He turned to face us, wearing jeans, a t-shirt and sandals. Behind a cage was a chair and a microphone, which I assumed he used to stay in touch with his drivers.

Before I could ask a question, Jerry said, "What did you mean 'more cops'?"

"I had the cops here today because one of my drivers is missin'," the man said.

Jerry and I exchanged a look.

"Where was his last pick up?" I asked.

"Henderson." He went behind the cage, looked at his records and read off an address.

"That's it," Jerry said. "That's the address."

"Then I guess you should be talkin' to the cops," the man said. "Your missin' a girl, I'm missin' a driver *and* a car."

"Look," I said, "what's your name?"

"Falco," he said.

"Falco, did you talk to a detective tonight?"

"I did," he said. "Some uniformed guys came when I called, but then they called for a detective, and two showed up."

"Do you remember their names?"

"Yeah," he said, "Detective Fields and Detective Owens."

I didn't know them, but thankfully one of the detectives wasn't Hargrove.

"Okay, can you call me at the Sands if you hear from your driver?"

He took down my number and said, "Sure."

"And whether you hear from him or not, Falco," I said, "give me a call if you ever want to go to a show at the Copa Room. You've got free tickets."

"Hey, wow, man," he said, "that's great. Thanks."

We left the office and got into the car.

"Are we goin' to the cops?" Jerry asked.

"As long as it's not Hargrove," I said. "But let's take a ride over to the Riv, first."

"Now?"

"Right now."

# Chapter Thirty-One

We drove to the Riviera and talked to all the valets out front. Some of them remembered Lake Mead cabs dropping people off in front, but none saw a beautiful, long-legged girl getting out of a cab—and they'd remember that.

None of them recalled seeing anything resembling a kidnapping in front of the Riv.

"People are jumping in and out of cabs all day, Eddie," one valet said. "We don't have any idea what happens after the cab pulls away."

"No, of course not," I said. I checked my watch. The Riviera showgirls would have come off stage by now, which means we could go inside and talk to their choreographer—their den mother.

"Let's go inside," I said to Jerry.

Sherry O'Neil had taken over the Riviera girls eighteen months ago, after having danced on the line herself for eight years. An injury took her off the line, and she worked her way up to her present job.

I found Sherry backstage, standing still while the girls ran back and forth, in various stages of undress.

"Geez," Jerry said, his eyes wide.

"Eddie!" Sherry said. "You missed the show."

"I'm sure it was great," I said.

Sherry was in her late thirties, would normally still be on the line if she hadn't injured herself. She still had a perfect dancer's body, and long blonde hair.

"Who's this big fella?" she asked.

"Sherry, this is Jerry Epstein, from Brooklyn."

"Hello, Jerry."

Jerry was still looking around at the girls, and mumbled, "Hi," to her.

"What's up, Eddie? What brings you here?"

"I'm looking for a girl named Gina."

"Gina?" she asked. "From your Sands Garden Cafe? I've been callin' her. Tryin' to get her in here to offer her a spot."

"She was on her way here today, Sherry," I said. "She never got here?"

"I haven't seen her," she said. "I can ask the other girls, but I doubt it. Is somethin' wrong?"

"She might be missin'," I said.

"Oh, my, that's . . . I was kinda mad when she didn't show, but if she's missin', that's terrible."

"Look, Sherry," I said, "can you keep the spot open for her?"

"I can't, Eddie," she said. "I had to put somebody on the line tonight, and she was great. I can't take the spot away from her if and when your Gina shows up."

"But if she's missin', and it's not her fault—"

"I tell you what I can do," Sherry said. "The next spot that opens is hers."

"That's great, Sherry."

"But then, you have to find her first, right?"

"Absolutely right." I gave her a hug. "Thanks, doll."

Jerry and I walked outside and back to his sedan. When we got into the front seat he asked, "Where to, Mr. G.?"

"I hate to say it," I said, "but I think we're gonna have to talk to the detectives."

"And what if we run into your guy, Hargrove?"

"If we do," I said, "I'm gonna act like I'm there to see him."

"With me along?"

"I think you might have to stay in the car, Jerry," I said. "I'm not gonna tell any of the detectives that you and Gina were working for Danny."

"What're you gonna tell them?"

"Just that she was renting a house in Henderson and took a cab to the Riviera, only she never got there."

"And what about Danny?"

"Yeah," I said, "we're gonna have to call Danny and bring him in on this."

"He's gonna be pissed at me," Jerry said.

"Yeah, he is," I said. "But if Gina snuck out, then he's gonna be pissed at her, too."

"So . . . where to?"

"I gave it another moment's thought, and then said, "You know what? My house."

***

When we got to my place, I grabbed two cans of Piels from the refrigerator, and tossed one to Jerry, who caught it one-handed. Then I tried Danny's place.

"What the fuck—" he said into his phone. "It's one a.m."

"Sorry, Danny, but we have a problem."

"Eddie? Who's we?"

"All of us. Jerry's here with me at my place."

"Where's Gina?"

"That's the problem."

Quickly, I explained that she had snuck out to go to the Riviera, and everything that had happened since then.

"Jesus, what was Jerry doin'?" he demanded.

"He told her not to go," I said, "but he couldn't sit on her."

"Yeah, yeah . . . you said you're at your house?"

"We were gonna go and talk to the detectives, but I decided to come here and give you a call first."

"Hold off on that, Eddie," Danny said. "I'm on my way over to you."

"Okay, but why—" I started but he hung up.

"Is he pissed?" Jerry asked, as I hung up.

"He is, but I think more at himself than you," I said.

Jerry drained his beer and crushed the can in his big hand.

"No, it's my fault," he said. "Whatever happens to her, I shoulda kept her safe. That was my job."

"Let's find her," I said, "and then nobody has to be blamed."

"If she's okay," Jerry said. "Maybe I should tell you what we were doin'—"

"I tell you what," I said, cutting him off. "Why don't we leave that to Danny? After all, it's his business."

"Okay," he said, "but if he doesn't tell ya, then I'm gonna. That's the only way we're gonna find 'er."

"Maybe the three of us can figure this out, without getting the police involved," I said.

"I'm always in favor of keepin' the cops out," Jerry said.

# Chapter Thirty-Two

When I opened the door, Danny was standing there with a bag.

"Chips and beer," he said. "I know you ain't been spendin' so much time home, lately."

"Thanks," I said, taking the bag from him.

The beer was more Piels, and the chips were potato.

In the living room, Jerry was sitting on my sofa, looking like a whipped dog.

"Relax, you big ape," Danny said. "It wasn't your fault. She snuck out on you."

"I shoulda kept a better eye on 'er."

"There you go," Danny said. "Why should I come down on you when you're gonna beat yourself up over this."

That didn't cheer Jerry up at all.

I tossed the bag of chips onto the kitchen table, went back to the living room with three beers and handed them out.

"Okay," Danny said, "I guess I better fill you in. Unless Jerry already has."

"Jerry hasn't said a word. That's totally up to you."

"I appreciate that, Jerry," Danny said.

"He's lyin'," Jerry said. "I was gonna tell 'im, but he stopped me. Said it should be you."

"Then I appreciate it from both of you," Danny said.

"So? Shoot," I said, sitting back in my chair.

"You know about the girls who've disappeared over the past few months?"

"Only what I've seen on TV and in the papers."

"Well, three women have gone missin'," Danny said. "And it looks like the cops have put them in a pending file."

"Damn cops are lazy," Jerry commented.

"I have a client who came to me to find his daughter, and I couldn't help as long as the cops were working the case. But when a few months went by and the cops put it in pending, the man came back to me, and I took the case."

"And you decided you needed bait?"

"All the girls were last seen on Fremont Street," Danny said. "That pissed me off. That's my street. So yeah, I decided to dangle some bait, out there. And when I saw Gina that day, I knew she was it."

"And you wanted Jerry for back up."

"Back up," Danny said, "and to keep an eye on Gina."

"But Gina has now disappeared from Henderson," I said. "Not Fremont Street."

"So either my guy has changed his M.O.," Danny said, "or she was taken by somebody else."

"Or," I said, "maybe she took off on her own."

"Why would she do that?" Jerry asked.

"Did this job scare her, Jerry?" I asked.

"No," the big guy said, "she knew me and Danny would keep her safe."

"And yet she snuck off by herself."

"To get that spot as a Riviera show girl," Jerry said. "That was her dream."

"She wouldn't have walked away from this job," Danny said. "We talked about it at the beginning. She felt bad for those girls and wanted to do something."

"So where do we look?" I said. "Her apartment?"

"That's a start," Danny said, "but if it's my guy and he took her from Henderson, then maybe he's gonna take her to Fremont Street."

"So we split up."

"Yeah," Danny said. "Eddie, you check her apartment, and Jerry and me, we'll go to Fremont Street."

"Okay," I said, "but what about the cops? Do you know Detectives Fields and Owens?"

"Yeah," Danny said, "they work missing persons. They're the idiots who have put these girls into their pending files."

"Well, the cab company called the cops," I said, "and the dispatcher spoke to Fields and Owens. So they're on this."

"They've been on it," Danny said. "They're not gonna find nothin'."

"Maybe," Jerry said, "they'll find the cabbie."

"That would be a big help," I admitted.

"Those two couldn't find their asses with both hands," Danny said.

"I'm just glad Hargrove's not involved," I said.

"Well . . ." Danny said.

"What?"

"Hargrove's been investigating a joker named Leo McKern," Danny said.

"So?"

"So I think McKern is involved with the missing girls," he said.

"You think he's grabbin' them?" I asked.

"I think he's workin' with whoever's grabbin' the girls," Danny said.

"And what are they doin' with them?" I asked.

"I'm thinkin' slave trade," Danny said. "Those girls are well out of the country, right now."

"How do you intend to find your client's daughter?" Jerry asked.

"First find the guy who took her, then find out who he sold her to. Then I'm gonna go and get her."

"You can count on me, if you want company," Jerry said. "And if you don't hold losin' Gina against me."

"Thanks, big guy," Danny said. "I might take you up on that. And we ain't lost her yet."

"I don't think there's much we can do tonight," I said, "but the sun'll be up in a few hours."

"I've got my car here," Danny said, "so I'll take Jerry with me and you can use his sedan. I know it's not a Caddy, but . . ."

"That's okay," I said. "Right now, the least of my concerns is what car I'm drivin'."

My caddy was in a body shop being worked on, and I tried not to think about it too much.

As Danny and Jerry went to the door Danny said, "If it's okay with you, I wanna hit Fremont Street now. It'll still be lit up."

"I'm with you," Jerry said. "You just lead the way."

"Eddie, we'll stay in touch," Danny said.

"Good luck, guys."

Once they were gone, I collected the empty beer cans and tossed them in the trash. I decided to get an hour or two of sleep before heading over to Gina's apartment, hoping I'd find her there.

# Chapter Thirty-Three

I woke after two hours and took a shower. I wasn't feeling refreshed, but what I had to do was waking me up. I called the Sands, got connected to the Garden Café and asked for Cassie. I knew she'd be working the breakfast shift.

"Eddie?" she said, coming on the line.

"Cassie, I don't have time to explain, but I need Gina's address."

"Sure," she said. "She lives at the Flamingo Arms Apartments on Flamingo Road. She's in number two-oh-two."

"Okay, thanks, Cass."

"I hope it helps."

"I'll let you know."

I hung up and went out to Jerry's sedan. I knew where the Flamingo Arms Apartment complex was. It was one of those with bikini bodies lounging around the pool. I was hoping one of them would be Gina, and she'd have an explanation for me.

It took me twenty minutes to get there. You can get almost anywhere in Vegas in twenty minutes. And they were building new highways that would get you around even faster.

When I pulled into the Flamingo Arms parking lot, the bikini babes were not around the pool. Apparently it was too early. But it was summer, so they'd be out there eventually.

I walked past the pool to the stairway up to the second level, found the door with two-oh-two on it. Now that I'd gotten this far, I hadn't thought about how to get inside. So I knocked. As expected, there was no answer.

But the door next to it opened and a pretty girl looked out.

"Are you lookin' for Gina?" she asked.

"I am."

"She hasn't been home in a few days," she said. "I was gettin' worried."

"Are you friends?"

"We're neighbors," she said, "but I like to think we're friends."

"What's your name?"

She stepped out so I could see her four-foot-ten frame was wearing a bikini. She looked all of twenty years old.

"Shari," she said, "Shari Sumner."

"Well, Shari, I was trying to figure out a way to get into Gina's apartment. You wouldn't have an answer for me, would you?"

"Who are you?"

"My name's Eddie, from the Sands. I'm trying to find Gina. She's missin'."

"Eddie G.?" she asked. "She's talked about you."

"Glad to hear it."

"Wait a minute."

She ran into her apartment, reappeared seconds later.

"We exchanged keys, in case one of us ever got locked out."

She held it out to me. When I reached for it, she pulled it back.

"Only if I can come in with you," she said.

"What would Gina say about that?"

"She gave me the key, didn't she? Besides, somebody has to make sure you don't steal anything."

"Deal," I said, and she handed me the key.

I unlocked the door and we went inside. I was surprised at how neat and clean the place was. The living room had nice furniture, just a little dust because she'd been away working with Danny, I guessed.

In the bedroom the bed was made, everything was in its place.

"It's been a few days since I've seen her, which explains the dust," Shari said. "Otherwise all the surfaces usually shine."

I stopped looking around and looked at her. Gina had never struck me as a neat freak.

"Yeah, I know," Shari said. "She's a neat freak."

"What are you, a mind reader?"

"I know what men are thinking."

"Aren't you a little young for that?" I asked. "Twenty?"

"That's nice," she said. "I'm twenty-six."

"Wow," I said, "I'm not usually that far off."

"I'll just say thanks. What are we lookin' for?"

"Well, first I was lookin' for Gina," I said, "now I'm lookin' for somethin' that might tell me where she is."

"Her phone book's in the kitchen."

"Let's try that."

Like the rest of the apartment, the kitchen was pristine. Not a stain in sight. There was a coffee pot on the stove. When I picked it up, it was empty, and clean.

"There," she said, pointing to the countertop.

It was one of those pop open phone books you usually saw in offices. Hit the letter you want and there's the page—only I didn't know which one to hit.

"Problem?"

"This isn't gonna help," I said. "Can you tell me where her family lives?"

"Sure," Shari said, "Boulder City."

"Really?"

"Where'd you think she was from?"

"I don't know, California?"

"Yeah, she looks like a California girl, with that blonde hair," Shari said. "Why are you lookin' for her, exactly."

I decided not to worry Shari too much.

"The Riviera's tryin' to find her."

Her eyes popped open.

"Did she get the job? On the line?"

"She did."

"Wow, good for her," she said, clapping her hands. "You know, she's been scared shitless about that."

"Why scared?"

"Time's runnin' out," Shari said. "She's twenty-nine."

She had no idea how true her statement about time was.

We went back to the living room.

"What about a boyfriend?"

"Nobody regular."

"Anybody she might be with now? At his place? A hotel?" I asked.

"I don't think so."

"Why not?"

"She woulda told me."

"You said you were more neighbors than friends."

"That was before I knew who you were," Shari said. "Besides, she gave me a key. We're friends, we talk."

"Well then," I said, "you can tell me her family's address."

# Chapter Thirty-Four

Shari gave me Gina's parents address in Boulder City. I thanked her for her help, gave her back the key and left. Still no bikinis around the pool. Maybe next time.

I wondered if I drove to Boulder City and talked to her family, if I'd be able to do it without panicking them. Probably not. But I needed to know if she was there. Gina may have left Jerry and that house in Henderson, not to go to the Riv, but to get away from a situation she no longer wanted to be involved in.

Boulder City was originally built in nineteen thirty-one for the specific reason of housing workers who were building Hoover dam. It had been a Company town, owned and run by the government until nineteen fifty-nine, when the town was incorporated. It was also only one of two cities in Nevada which prohibited gambling. (The other was Panaca, Nevada's first permanent settlement, founded by Mormons in eighteen sixty-four).

I went over several scenarios in my head before pulling the car to a stop in front of Gina's parents' house. I got out of the car and made my way up the walk to the front door of the one family, ranch style home. I rang the doorbell and waited.

When the door was opened, it was obviously Gina's mother. She wasn't blonde, but she was tall and long-legged, like her daughter. She must've had Gina young, because her daughter was twenty-nine, but she didn't look a day over forty-five.

"Can I help you?"

"Mrs.—" I groped for a minute for Gina's last name, and then it came. "—Reynolds?"

"Yes, that's right."

"My name is Eddie Gianelli, Ma'am," I said. "I work at the Sands."

"Are you a friend of my daughter's?"

"Yes, I am."

"Come in, then, Mr. Gianelli."

She backed away from the door, allowing me to enter.

"Now that I think of it, I've heard her mention your name. They call you Eddie G., right?"

"That's right."

"Come into the living room and meet my husband."

I followed her through the neat and tidy house. It was easy to see where Gina got her neat freakiness from. All the surfaces I passed gleamed.

"Edward," she said, as we entered the living room, "this is Mr. Gianelli, from the Sands. He's a friend of Gina's."

Edward Reynolds stood and extended his hand. He looked ten years older than his wife, but was also tall and slender, like his wife and daughter.

"Mr. Gianelli," he asked, "what can we do for you?"

"Edward," his wife said, "let me at least offer Mr. Gianelli some coffee."

"Miriam," he said, "let's find out why he's here."

"It's all right, Mrs. Reynolds," I said, "I don't need anything."

"There, see?" Edward said. "Have a seat, Mr. Gianelli and tell us why you're here. Is my daughter all right?"

"To be honest, sir," I said, "I was sort of hoping she was here."

"What?" Miriam said. "Why would she be here?"

"Well," I said, "we haven't seen her for a couple of days. I checked her apartment and her neighbor hasn't seen her, either."

"Maybe she took some time off," Edward said. "Went away with a girlfriend? Or boyfriend?"

"That's what I've been thinking," I said, "but I need to find her, to give her a message."

"What message?" he asked.

"The Riviera has a spot open on their line," I said. "They've been trying to get ahold of her."

Miriam's hands went to her mouth.

"The showgirl spot?" she asked. "Gina's been waiting for that."

"I know," I said, "and I don't want her to lose it."

"Well," Edward said, "she's not here."

"Would you know the name of a girlfriend or boy-friend she might have gone away with?" I noticed my Brooklyn accent hid when I was talking to certain people, like these. How should I put it? Nice people?

"Miriam?" Edward asked, deferring to his wife on this point.

"I'm sorry, no," she said. "I don't know—she hasn't mentioned a boy, and she has several girlfriends—mostly at work. Like Cassie."

"I've spoken to Cassie," I said. "In fact, she's the one who took the message from the Riviera, and then came to me. Neither of us wants to see her lose this chance."

"Well," Edward said, "if she went off gallivanting somewhere without telling her friends, her family, or her boss, then maybe she should lose it."

"Edward!"

"I'm going to go to the den, Miriam," he said. "Why don't you see Mr. Gianelli to the door?" He nodded at me and left the room.

"I'm sorry," Miriam Reynolds said, "but my husband doesn't approve of showgirls. He doesn't want his daughter being one."

"I understand."

"I'll see you to the door."

She walked me to the door and, as she opened it, she put her hand on my arm.

"Should I be worried about my daughter, Mr. G.?"

"No, ma'am," I lied. "I'll find her and get the message to her."

She gripped my arm tighter.

"She's not an irresponsible child, Mr. G. . . ."

"I know that, Miriam." I patted her hand. "I'll find her."

I walked back to the car, feeling like shit.

\*\*\*

I promised Miriam Reynolds I'd find her daughter. Meanwhile, I didn't have the faintest idea where to look. I only hoped Danny and Jerry would have some luck on Fremont Street.

I went back to the Sands, wondering if I should've driven to the police and talked to the detectives. But if I did that, I might run into Hargrove. I wasn't ready to go head-to-head with him, yet. I decided to give it more thought before I did that. After all, I was going to have to call him a liar.

I parked behind the building and entered the back way. I stopped at the front desk, just to check for messages. Apparently Jerry Lewis had not yet been contacted by his blackmailer. That, or he had elected to go on his own. Either way, I didn't need that distraction right now.

I was also hoping there'd be a message from Danny or Big Jerry, but there wasn't.

I was lost.

I started away from the desk when one of the clerk's called out, "Hey, Eddie!"

I turned and looked at him. He held up his telephone receiver.

"Call for you."

"Who is it?"

"Some guy named Falco."

The cab dispatcher.

"I'll take it."

I grabbed the receiver from him.

"Falco? Eddie G. You callin' for those tickets?"

"Only if lettin' you talk to my driver deserves them," Falco said.

"He's back?"

"He's back."

## Chapter Thirty-Five

I drove to the garage of the Lake Mead Cab Company, parked down the street and made my way to the office. Falco was sitting behind his cage, speaking to one of his drivers on the microphone. He waved as I came in.

When he put the microphone down, he stood up.

"Where is he?"

"In our break room," Falco said. "I'll take you there."

He led me down a long hallway.

"How did you find him?" I asked.

"I didn't," Falco said. "He walked back in here."

"How did he get away from whoever took him?"

"I'll let him tell you that."

"Have you called the police?"

"No, I thought I'd call you first. Besides, I have my driver back, and he knows where my car is. I'm good."

We came to a door and he opened it. Inside a disheveled man was sitting at a long table, with a can of Coke and a bag of chips in front of him. He was in the act of stuffing his mouth as we entered.

"Eddie, this is Morty, my driver," Falco said. "Morty, Eddie is from the Sands Casino. The girl you picked up works for him."

Morty finished chewing, washed down the chips with a mouthful of soda.

"How are you?" I asked.

"I'm okay."

"Can you tell me what happened after you picked up the girl in Henderson?"

"I guess . . ."

"Okay.

He looked at Falco, who said, "Tell 'im."

"She wanted to go to the Riviera. I drove her there. When I pulled up in front, a man jumped into the front seat and pointed a gun at me."

He stopped, swallowed nervously.

"Then what happened?"

"He told me to drive away. The girl started to talk, but he pointed the gun at her and told her to shut up."

"And then?"

"He had me drive to a deserted area on Paradise Road and pull over. Then he made me get out, told the girl if she got out, he'd shoot her." He sipped from his soda can.

"What then?"

"He made me get in the trunk."

"And?"

"That was it."

"Tell me what you heard while you were in the trunk."

"H-he took the girl out of the back seat. They argued for a short time, then I heard another vehicle drive up, doors open and close, the girl screamed, and then they drove away."

"That's it?"

"That's all I know."

"How did you get out?"

"It took me all night. I just kept kicking at the trunk until it finally popped open. When I got out, I could barely walk, but I made my way to a busier street." He laughed. "I actually took a cab here."

"Okay," I said. "Do you have any idea where they might have taken her?"

"None."

"Or what direction they might've gone?"

"No, sorry."

"When the other car pulled up, did anyone say anythin'?"

"I heard some talk, but couldn't make out the words."

"Male voices?"

"Yes."

"How many?"

Morty thought a moment.

"Two," he said, "it sounded like two."

"You didn't catch any words?"

Morty closed his eyes.

"I can't—"

"Just think about it Morty," I said. "See if anythin' comes to you."

Morty closed his eyes, stuffed some chips into his mouth.

I looked at Falco.

"You sure you don't wanna call the cops?"

"Those two detectives?" He snorted. "They didn't do shit, did they?"

"No, not yet," I said.

"Then why call 'em?" he asked, "Like I said, I've got my driver and car back. I'm havin' a tow truck go and get it, now."

"Right now?"

"Yes. It's probably on its way here."

"I'd like to take a look at it."

"Sure," Falco said. "As soon as it comes in. Look, I got to get back to my station."

"Sure," I said. "Just let me know when that car gets here."

"Will do."

Falco left the room. I turned, saw Morty tearing open another bag of chips.

"You get hungry locked in a trunk all night," he said, with a shrug.

I looked around.

Robert J. Randisi

"Where are the vending machines?"

# Chapter Thirty-Six

I was finishing up a bag of chips and a Coke when Falco stuck his head in the room.

"The car just got dropped off."

"Great."

I followed him down the hall to the garage.

"That's it," he said, pointing at a cab that sat in the center of the garage.

"It looks okay," I said. "Why did it have to be towed?"

"Somebody pulled the distributor cap."

"Seems to me Morty would've heard that."

"Maybe. I've gotta go back to work."

"I'll have a look, tell you when I'm done."

"Okay."

I walked over to the cab, saw that the trunk was open, and the lid was dented where Morty had kicked it.

I checked the front seat, because that's where Morty said the guy with the gun sat. I stuck my fingers down the back of the seat, looked on the floor. What was I looking for? A matchbook? Maybe a napkin from a bar he drank in? Or how about a piece of paper with his address on it?

Just for the heck of it, I checked the back seat, where Gina had been sitting. I ran my hand along the back of the seat, was about to give up when the tips of my fingers touched something. I reached down further, grabbed it and pulled it out. Okay, yes, it was a matchbook, but who knew how long it had been there?

I held it up. It actually didn't look all that old. The front was very bright and lurid and said THE CAROUSEL CASINO. I knew where that was. It used to be called The Silver Palace until it was sold in nineteen sixty-four. It was right next door to the Girls of Glitz and Glam Strip Club. Both were located in a section that was called Glitter Gulch, because of all the neon there. And Glitz and Glam was actually on Fremont Street—where Jerry and Danny were looking for Gina.

Coincidence?

I decided it wasn't. I decided that Gina had stuffed that matchbook down into the seat as a message. I pocketed the matchbook and got out of the car.

Instead of going back to the front to tell Falco I was leaving, I went back to the break room, where Monty was still sitting.

"Aren't you gonna go home?" I asked.

"Soon as my feet don't hurt so much," he said, "and my legs stop shakin'."

"Well, while you're still here," I said, "when's the last time you took a fare to the Carousel Casino down on Fremont Street?"

"Huh? Long time. I hate it down there. It's sleazy."

Morty looked pretty sleazy himself, but of course he'd spent a whole night in the trunk of a cab.

"Falco says the distributor cap was removed from your cab."

He looked surprised.

"Oh yeah! I heard the hood open. That musta been when they done it."

"So do you remember anythin' else?"

"Just one thing," he said.

"What's that?'

"A word."

Now it was getting like pulling teeth.

"What word, Morty?"

"Well, when the other car pulled up and they started talking, I couldn't make everythin' out—well, anythin' really, they were talkin' so fast, and one guy was really mad—"

"Oh my God!" I snapped. "What was the word you heard, Morty?"

"Uh, Fremont," Morty said. "Somebody said 'Fremont.'"

The matchbook started to burn a hole in my pocket.

# Chapter Thirty-Seven

I parked the car behind the Four Queens Casino, which had opened last month. That made it the newest looking casino in an area that looked run down, at best. It was only at night, when the neon came on, that it got better.

I walked around to the front, which put me right on Fremont Street near Second Avenue, across from the Golden Nugget. Binion's Horseshoe was between Main and First, while Danny's office was on the same side of the street as Binion's, between First and Second Street. Even from there I could see and hear the forty-foot neon cowboy named Vegas Vic, who waved and said "Howdy, Pardner" from atop the Pioneer, on Casino Drive.

The Carousel and the Girls of Glitz and Glam were near First. That put them down the street from Binion's.

I didn't expect to find Danny in his office. I thought he and Jerry would be on the street, tryin to catch sight of Gina. If the man who had already grabbed three girls had also grabbed her, he'd have to keep his connection to Fremont Street by bringing her down here. If he had already done that, then Danny and Jerry might spot her. If he had already done it.

Whoever had picked up Gina and the man with the gun on Paradise Road, might have gone somewhere else first. Maybe to where they kept the girls after whisking them off Fremont Street.

Putting Morty in the trunk of the car told us one thing about the man. We didn't know if he was killing the girls, or selling them, but at least we knew that he didn't kill men. Or Morty would be dead.

I could walk up and down the street looking for Jerry and Danny—or Gina, for that matter—but that didn't work for finding out what she knew. After that I'd take a walk to the Carousel and see what was there.

I went to Danny's office, opened the door and hurried up the stairs two at a time. When I opened the door, Penny was standing up, her eyes wide.

"Jesus," she said, "I thought maybe somebody was chasing Danny up the stairs."

"He's not here?" I asked.

She sat back down behind her desk.

"No. And I'm worried, about both of them."

"I saw them last night," I said, and told her what had happened.

"So they're down here somewhere on the street, looking for her?"

"Yes, but they don't know what I know," I said. "I've got to go and look at the Carousel. If you hear anything, tell them I'm there."

"Okay. But what's there?"

"I hope Gina," I said. "I found this in the back seat of the cab she was in." I showed her the matchbook.

"That could've already been there."

"Could've been," I said, "but it looks new to me."

"Eddie," she said, "think about it. Why would she be carrying that matchbook? From that place?"

"I don't know," I said, "but it's all I've got."

"A-all right," she said. "If they call, or come in, I'll tell 'em."

"Thanks. I'll see you later."

"You better," she said. "I don't want to have to worry about you, too."

"Don't," I said, and headed back down the stairs.

*** 

During the day you could see the soot and decay of Fremont Street. Vegas was mostly concerned with the strip. Downtown needed a definite overhaul.

I walked down the street to the Carousel Casino and stopped outside. It had so much color out front—and neon at night—that it looked cheap and gaudy rather than festive—unlike, say, The Flamingo. And the clientele fit.

The Carousel was a small casino, but its floor had all the activity of the larger ones—blackjack, roulette, wheel of fortune, slots—all crammed into a small space. And even at this early hour of the day, a lot of people pissing away their hard earned—or stolen—money with looks of desperation on their sweaty faces.

I walked through the casino, keeping an eye out for Gina, even though I knew she wouldn't be there. At least, not on the casino floor. If she was here, she was being held in a back room.

There were two security guards on the floor, one pit boss, one cigarette girl. The cigarette girl seemed to be my best bet.

"Cigars, cigarettes . . ." she was saying as she approached me. "Hey, Eddie G."

"You know me?" I said.

"I do," she said. "But you don't remember me."

She was about five-five, long black hair, pale skin, and looked like a lot of cigarette girls who passed through the Sands.

"You worked at the Sands."

"Bingo," she said. "For about a week. Then I got fired."

"For . . ."

"Bein' a pickpocket."

"Suspected pickpocket?"

"Oh, no," she said, "I did it. That's why I'm not mad at you."

"I fired you?"

"Not exactly."

"How long have you worked here?" I asked.

"Coupla months," she said. "They don't care if I pick pockets, so long as I sell a lot of ciggies. What are you doin' here?"

"Lookin' for a girl."

She popped her eyes at me.

"You found me. Gloria."

"I'm lookin' for a girl named Gina," I said. "Works at the Garden Café."

"Did she work there when I did?"

"No."

"Then I don't know her."

"No," I said, "but maybe you saw a girl bein' brought in here against her will? Blonde, long legs?"

"A showgirl? I hate showgirls."

"A waitress, remember?"

"Oh, yeah. Why would somebody force her to come here? Check that—lots of girls have to be forced to come here. But why her?"

"How much do you have invested in this job?" I asked.

"That depends," she said. "Can you get me back into the Sands?"

"No," I said, "but I can get you into the Flamingo, or the Riv."

"Deal. Whataya need?"

\*\*\*

I got myself around to the back of the Carousel and waited. Before long the back door opened, and Gloria peered out and waved at me.

"Come on!"

I hurried over and she let me in. We were at the end of a long hallway, with doors on either side.

"Okay," I said, "you go back to work."

"You're gonna call me, right?" She'd already given me her phone number.

"I am," I said. "I promise."

She kissed me, suddenly, and brushed my crotch with her hand.

"And I want more than just another job from you."

She turned and ran down the hall.

# Chapter Thirty-Eight

I moved down the hall and started checking doors, hoping against hope I'd open one and see Gina sitting there. I was praying that the matchbook in the back seat had brought me here for a reason—the right reason.

Of course, it wasn't going to be that easy. The first door I tried was locked. I tried to turn the doorknob again, without jiggling the door and warning anyone inside. In my experience, locked doors usually had somebody on the other side.

I moved on, found several unlocked doors, and opened them carefully. I found an empty storeroom, a closet, and a bathroom. Gina wasn't in any of them.

I found another locked door, but before I could make a decision about what to do, the main door that lead to the casino opened. The only place I had to go was the closet, so I ducked inside.

I heard the door open and somebody entered the hall. I was just hoping they weren't coming to the closet. They walked past, so I was able to open the door a crack and peer out. I saw a man walk to one of the locked doors, unlock it with a key, and enter. I left the closet and went to the door, pressed my ear to it. I heard voices—two men, and a woman. Was the woman Gina? And if it was, what could I do? Burst in? With no weapon?

I needed my big buddy, Jerry.

***

I hated to do it, but I left by the back door, went back around to the front and found Gloria, still selling cigarettes. As I entered, she saw me and rushed over.

"Was she there?"

"I don't know," I said. "I found two locked doors. A man came into the hall and I had to hide in a closet."

"That was Preston, the manager. I saw him go back there and I almost yelled."

"He used a key and went into one of the locked rooms. I listened at the door, thought I heard a woman, but I can't be sure. Do you have any idea what the locked doors lead to?"

"Offices," she said. "One is Preston's, one belongs to the owner, but he's never here."

"I need to go and get some help and come back," I said. "Can you keep an eye out for me?"

"I'll see if they bring her through here," she said, "but what if they go out the back?"

"If I can keep them from going out the back, they'd have to come through here."

"How would you do that?"

"There are dumpsters back there," I said. "Maybe I can put one in front of the back door. It opens out, so that would block it. They'd have to come through here."

"Or walk around and move the dumpster," she offered.

"You're too smart to be a cigarette girl," I said.

"Tell that to somebody when you get me a new job," she said.

"Okay," I said, "I'm gonna start by blockin' the door, and then go from there."

"What do you want me to do in the meantime?"

"Just watch, listen, and stay safe," I said. "Don't do anything dangerous."

"All right, Eddie," she said. "But you better hurry back."

She was right about that.

***

Back behind the building, I looked at the dumpsters. There were several and they were different sizes. One was metal, too big and heavy for me to move. But one was made of rubber. It was heavy, but had wheels, so I was able to move it. I rolled it over to the door and placed it there sideways. They'd be able to open it maybe an inch, but they wouldn't be able to see what was blocking it.

That done, I ran back to Fremont Street. If Jerry was anywhere on that street, I'd find him.

# Chapter Thirty-Nine

Oddly, I thought this must be what a chicken without a head felt like. I started running down Fremont Street, eyes peeled for Big Jerry somewhere along the way. But by the time I reached Danny's office, I still hadn't spotted either one of them.

I ran up the stairs, this time managing not to scare Penny, who simply looked up at me from her desk.

"They called," she said. "They're down the street, near Fifth. They found something and said they'd wait for you there, near the El Cortez."

I thanked her and ran out.

\*\*\*

The El Cortez opened in nineteen forty-one. One of the oldest properties in Vegas. Bugsy Seigel and Meyer Lansky bought it in forty-five, and the Jackie Guaghan bought it in sixty-three. Gaughan owned several casinos, and it's said that, at one point, he owned twenty-five per cent of Vegas.

I found Danny and Jerry standing right in front of the El Cortez.

"There you are," Danny said. "I was about to send Jerry to the pay phone, again."

"Whataya got?" I asked.

"We got word that Leo McKern might have a room in the El Cortez."

"So what are you gonna do, search the whole hotel?" I asked.

"I thought we'd sit in the lobby and wait," Danny said.

"And what about Gina?"

"If we catch McKern, maybe he'll tell us where Gina is."

"I got a better idea," I said, and told them about the matchbook, and the Carousel.

"So you think she's there now?" Danny asked.

"I think she could be," I said. "I've got somebody watchin', but she's not going to be able to do anythin' if they start to leave."

Danny looked at the El Cortez, then down the street toward the Carousel.

"Okay," he said, "let's try the Carousel first."

We headed that way, but when we came to his office he said, "Hang on. I gotta go up and get somethin'."

He ran up the stairs and I looked at Jerry.

"I'm heeled, but he ain't," Jerry said. "He's gettin' his piece."

"You got your forty-five?"

He grinned.

"What else?"

Danny came running back down, his gun in a holster on his belt, now. He also held out some pink slips of messages in his hand.

"Penny asked me to give you these," he said.

I usually left contact numbers at the front desk of the Sands hotel in case I got an important call. One was my house, and one was Danny's office. He loaned me Penny to take the messages.

"Anything important?" he asked, as I read them.

There were several, all from Jerry Lewis and Sammy Davis. Apparently, Lewis' blackmailer had called, and he was desperate to find me.

"Fuck," I said.

"What?" Danny asked.

I told him.

"Whatayou wanna do?" he asked.

I had to choose between Gina and Jerry Lewis. I would've chosen Gina in a heartbeat, but if anything happened to Jerry Lewis, I'd have helluva lot of explaining to do to Jack Entratter.

So Danny decided for me.

"Look, you go back to the Sands and take care of your Jerry Lewis problem. Jerry and me, we'll go over to the Carousel and check it out."

"There's a cigarette girl there named Gloria, a pretty brunette," I told him. "She's helping me. She let me in the back door, and she's watchin' to see if they take Gina out through the casino."

"The casino?" Jerry asked. "Why not the back door?"

"I blocked it with a dumpster," I said. "They're not gonna be able to open it."

"Okay, Gloria," Danny said, "got it."

"Take care of her," I said. "I'm gonna get her a better job when this is all over."

"Count on it," Danny said. "We better all get goin'."

"Good luck," I said.

I hated leaving the rescue of Gina to Danny and Jerry, but then she had been working with them when she was taken, and it was their responsibility. But if anything happened to her, I was going to feel lousy, because I had given the okay for Danny to recruit her.

I hightailed it to the Four Queens parking lot and drove Jerry's borrowed sedan back to the Sands.

# Chapter Forty

When I got to the Sands, it was early evening. I checked in with a clerk at the front desk, who had a few more messages for me, also from Jerry Lewis and Sammy. I called Sam, first.

"Where the hell you been, man?" Sammy squawked. "Jerry's been goin' crazy, man! He's been tryin' to find you, and he won't tell me why."

"I know why, Sam," I said. "Don't worry. I'll go and see him."

"Look," Sammy said, "don't be put off by his attitude, okay?"

"I've dealt with lots of attitudes over the past few years, Sammy."

"Yeah, well, Jerry's a button pusher," Sammy said.

"I'll keep my buttons under wraps."

"And lemme know what gives, huh?" Sammy asked. "I mean, if not details, then just . . . somethin'."

"I'll fill you in on what I can, Sam," I promised.

I hung up with him and called Jerry. He answered the phone and spoke very calmly. Too calm.

"I've been trying to find you," he said.

"I'm here," I said. "On my way up."

He hung up.

\*\*\*

I took the elevator to his floor. When I knocked on the door, he opened it, stared at me for a moment with no expression, then turned and walked away. When I entered and closed the door, he was seated on the couch.

"He called," he said.

"Called?" I said. "He didn't send a note?"

"No, he called on the phone."

"Has he ever done that before?"

"No," Lewis said, "I've never spoken to him before." He had his leg crossed over his knee, and his foot was going a mile a minute, flashing a red sock at me.

"When did he call?"

"Last night. I've been trying to find you all day."

I ignored the complaint.

"How did he sound?"

"How did he *sound*?" His mouth moved, as if he was chewing something. Sometimes I thought it was gum, but other times I knew there was nothing there. It was just like a tic. "He sounded like a sonofabitch who's trying to get fifty thousand dollars out of me."

"Did he tell you when and where?"

"This time he just told me how much," Jerry said. "He's supposed to call today with details."

"So we're still waitin'."

"*I'm* still waiting," Lewis said. "I don't know what you're doing."

"What I'm tryin' to do," I said, "is save a girl's life."

"Isn't that a job for the cops?"

"Not the cops in this town."

"Well," he said, "it looks like we're both trying to do an end run around the police."

"Let's just say I don't have a great relationship with, or opinion of, the detectives in this town."

"Good," Lewis said, "that proves I'm making the right decision by dealing with this myself . . . and with you."

"Well," I said, "we're going to see about that."

I wasn't happy. I had left Fremont Street when there was a chance to find Gina, just to come here and talk to an angry, non-funny, funnyman.

"Do you want me to sit around here and wait with you?" I asked.

His foot started going even faster.

"I just want to be able to find you when this next call comes in," he said. "Is that too much to ask? I mean, you offered your help, right? I didn't ask for it."

I couldn't have argued with that if I wanted to.

"Oh, and one more thing," he said, while I was on my way to the door. I turned and looked at him. "I'd like you to get me the fifty grand."

# Chapter Forty-One

I left Jerry Lewis, promising to stay in steady contact. I stopped at Jack Enratter's office. His girl wasn't there, but he was.

"Fifty grand?" he demanded. "What the hell does Jerry Lewis want with fifty grand?"

"He can afford it," I said, "he just wants us to front it. He'll pay it back."

"Jesus Christ, these hollywood guys!" he complained. "They're worse than gangsters."

"You oughtta know," I said. "You deal with both."

"Is this important?" he demanded.

"It's important to him."

He made a disgusted noise with his mouth and then said, "Yeah, I'll get him the money. You can pick it up at the cages."

***

Down in the lobby, I used a house phone to call Penny to see if she heard from Danny and Jerry.

"Nothing yet," she said. "I'm worried. I mean . . . it was just down the street."

"That's what I'm thinkin'," I said. "They should've been back by now."

"And Eddie?" she said. "I heard police sirens a little while ago."

"Damn it!"

I hung up and headed out, again.

\*\*\*

When I got down to the Carousel, there were cop cars and an ambulance in the alley behind it. I double parked and ran over to the mouth of the alley, where there was a crowd. Standing head-and-shoulders above the others was Jerry. As I reached him, I saw Danny next to him.

"What's going on?" I demanded.

"Eddie," Danny said, taking hold of my arms, "take it easy. They found the body of a young woman in the big dumpster."

"Is it Gina?" I asked.

"We don't know, yet."

"Shitshitshit!" I swore. "I knew I shouldn't've left."

"There was nothin' you could've done," Danny said. "We were still inside when we heard a man shoutin'. They called the cops, and we had to back off."

"Did you get a look into those locked rooms?" I asked.

"Look," Danny said, "let's back off and I'll tell you what happened. Jerry, keep watchin' and tell us if they identify the girl."

"Sure thing."

Danny and I left the crowd and crossed the street to my double-parked sedan.

"Park it legally so we don't get chased."

I found a spot on the street, just down from the Carousel, where Jerry would be able to find us.

"Okay," I said, turning off the motor, "shoot."

"After we left you, we went into the Carousel . . ."

\*\*\*

Danny and Jerry entered the Carousel, and immediately saw Gloria, the cigarette girl.

"Cigars, cigarettes—" she started as they approached her.

"I don't smoke," Jerry said, cutting her off.

"Good for you, big guy," she said. "Chewing gum?"

"Are you Gloria?" Danny asked.

"That's right, handsome," she said, with a flirtatious look. "Do I know you? I'd like to."

"Eddie G. sent us."

Her face changed at that point, became very serious.

"Where is he? Is he comin' back?" she asked.

183

"He can't right now," Danny said. "That's why we're here. Have you seen anythin'?"

"They haven't left yet, as far as I know," she said. "At least, nobody's come through the casino."

"And they haven't gone out the back?" Danny asked.

"I don't know if they tried," she said. "But I haven't heard any complaints."

Danny got an idea at that point.

"Jerry, go around back, see if the dumpster Eddie put against the door is still there. If it is, move it. I'll let you in. That way we'll know if they're still here."

"Got it," Jerry said. He turned and went out the front door.

"He's a big guy," she said. "Is he big . . . all over?"

"I don't wanna know," Danny said. "Where's the door to the hallway?"

"You can't go in there," she said. "You don't work here."

"But you can?"

"There's a room back there that us girls use to change in," she explained. "So nobody looks twice when I go back there . . . normally."

"Okay," he said, "so you go back and let Jerry in, but I've gotta get back there, too."

"To get a look in the locked rooms?"

"Yes."

"Well," she said, "I gotta tell you, Preston is still back there."

"Preston?"

"The manager," she said. "He's in his office."

"So if I ask to see him, I can get back there?" he said. She shrugged.

"Maybe."

"Who do I ask?"

She looked around, then pointed at a tall man standing off to one side. He was wearing a suit, hands clasped in front of him.

"That's Jackson, the pit boss on duty. Ask him."

"Okay," he said. "You go back, let Jerry in, and then let me know when you've done it."

"Okay," she said, "here goes."

According to Danny, he watched Gloria go through the door and waited for her to come back out again, only she never did. Then there was some kind of uproar from the back. At that point, Jerry came back in and joined Danny.

"What's happenin'?" Danny asked him.

"There was no dumpster against the door," Jerry said. "When I got back there, the door opened and a man came out carrying some bags of garbage. He went to the big dumpster, opened it, tossed his bags in, looked again and started yelling. Then he turned and ran back through the door. Before I could go over to the dumpster to see what scared him, he came back out with a couple of more men. They looked into the dumpster, then two men stayed by it while the other one went inside. I think he's callin' the cops."

As they watched, the door opened and a man stepped out, waved at the pit boss and called him over.

"Where's the cigarette girl?" Jerry asked.

"She went in there and hasn't come out."

"She didn't come out the back," Jerry said.

"So she's still there, somewhere."

The pit boss stepped through the door with the other man, and it closed.

"Let's go," Danny said.

"Where?"

"I still want a look in that hallway."

They hurried across the room, with only a few people paying any attention . . .

# Chapter Forty-Two

Danny continued with his story as more people began to gather at the mouth of the alley . . .

***

He and Jerry opened the door and stepped through. The hallway was empty. The door at the end had been propped open, and they could see activity outside.

"Let's find these locked doors Eddie talked about," Danny said.

They did, two of them. Jerry opened one with a shoulder, and another with a powerful kick.

"Nobody reacted," Danny said. "They were too busy out back."

"And what did you see?" I asked.

"Nothin'," Danny said. "They were both offices, with tables and a desk. But one of them had a chair that was in the center of the room."

"Like maybe somebody was tied to it?" I asked.

"It was a wooden chair, and there were scrapes on the back," Danny said. "I'd say somebody was handcuffed to it."

"Shit!" I swore.

"We went back out the front as we heard sirens and circled the building to see what was happening. That's when you found us."

It seemed right. I wasn't gone all that long, just back to the Sands to talk to Jerry Lewis, then came right back.

"Danny, we've gotta find out who's in that dumpster," I said. "It could be Gina, or Gloria."

"The cigarette girl?" He shook his head. "There was no time. Jerry was still in the back when she went through the door to the hallway. She said there was a changing room back there for the girls. My bet is she ducked into there when the commotion started and stayed. She might even still be there, now. But she's had plenty of time to get out."

"Maybe she's back in the casino."

"I'll go and have a look," Danny said. "You go back to Jerry."

We got out of the car and split up.

***

Jerry looked at me when I came up alongside him.

"You're just in time," he said. "They got somebody out of the dumpster and put 'em on a stretcher. They're gonna wheel 'em out."

"Was it a girl?"

"I couldn't tell."

As they wheeled the body toward us and the crowd parted, Danny came running back.

"It's not Gloria," he said. "She's fine."

"Then it could be Gina," I said.

"I hope not," Jerry said.

Behind the attendants with the gurney came two plain clothes detectives, neither of which were Hargrove, or the two from missing persons.

"Thank God Hargrove didn't catch this one," I said. "Let's see if we can get a look at the body."

"Let me do it," Danny said. "I know one of those attendants."

"Fine." Jerry and I stayed with the crowd, blending in as well as we could, given Jerry's height and bulk.

Danny ran over to the waiting ambulance, was standing there when the attendants reached it. He shook hands with one of them, who then uncovered the face for Danny to see. At that point the detectives reached the ambulance, gave the attendant an earful and shooed Danny away.

As they loaded the body into the back, Danny came trotting over.

"Is it Gina?" Jerry asked, anxiously.

"No," Danny said, then looked at me. "You're not gonna believe this."

"What?"

"It's not a girl," Danny said. "It's Leo McKern."

# Chapter Forty-Three

"Leo McKern," I said, shaking my head.

We were back at Danny's office, drinking the coffee that Penny had been nice enough to make for us before she left for the day. Danny took out a bottle of bourbon to sweeten the brew.

"She's a great girl," he said, "but her coffee needs help." He raised his eyebrows at both of us, and we each held our cups out.

"I'm glad it wasn't Gina," Jerry said, "but McKern was the guy we thought took her, and now he's dead. So what do we do next?"

"We still have to find 'er," Danny said. "And McKern was probably killed by a partner, or employer."

"But why?" Jerry asked.

Danny shrugged.

"A fallin' out, I'd guess."

"McKern was your key suspect, right?" I asked. "And he's the guy Hargrove was after."

"Right."

"So now what?" I asked. "You got anymore suspects?"

"Not a one," Danny said "McKern was my only connection."

"And who gave you him?"

"Just an informant."

"So what about your informant?" I asked. "Could he be involved?"

"No," he said. "I've used him for a long time. He keeps his ear to the ground for me."

"Okay, so how was McKern killed?" I asked. "Could you tell?"

"His throat had been cut," Danny said. "I saw that much."

"That's not a pro hit, then," I said. A professional would've tapped him once on the back of the head.

"Naw," Danny said, "somebody had it in for him. When you cut somebody's throat, you want them thinkin' about it as they're choking on their own blood."

"So okay," I said, "we've got three missing girls, now Gina, and a dead Leo McKern. So finally its murder."

"Hargrove is gonna be on both our asses after this," Danny said.

I snapped my fingers.

"What?"

"The cab driver," I said. "Let's show him a picture of Leo, see if he's the guy who snatched Gina and him with his cab,"

"The cab driver's back?" Danny asked. "I thought he'd turn up dead."

"I didn't tell you that?" I asked. "When I told you about the matchbook?"

"You found the matchbook in the back seat of the cab, you said," Danny reminded me, "I figured they found the car, but you didn't say they found the driver."

"Sorry," I said. "I guess I didn't get to that."

"That's okay, Mr. G.," Jerry said. "You got a lot on your mind."

"The Jerry Lewis thing?" Danny asked.

"It's comin' to a head," I said. "Anyway, the cabbie walked into his garage. His name's Morty. Now all we need is a picture of Leo McKern."

"I'll find one," Danny said. "Then I'll get over to Lake Mead Cab and show it to him. If it wasn't Leo, at least I'll get a description."

"Okay," I said, standing up. "I'm gonna leave findin' Gina to you, because you're the P.I., and I have no idea where to look anymore."

"Don't be hard on yourself," Danny said. "You got us to the Carousel."

"Yeah, I did, didn't I?" I said. "Just not in time."

I headed for the door, then stopped and turned.

"Wait," I said. "Do I get to ask now why you had Jerry and Gina set up in a house in Henderson?"

"Sure," he said. "The other three girls who are missing? They all lived in Henderson. Where else would I dangle bait?"

"Where else, indeed," I said, and left.

## Chapter Forty-Four

When I got back to the Sands, I could hear Jerry Vale singing in the lounge, so didn't go there. Vic Damone, yes; Steve Lawrence, definitely; Julius La Rosa, sure; even Al Martino. But Jerry Vale? No thanks.

It was late, so the offices on the fourth floor were closed including Jack Entratter's. Sometimes I'd sit in there after everyone was gone, but not tonight. I stopped at the hotel desk to see if Jerry Lewis had tried to get me. He had. One message. I called his suite, even though it was late.

"Did I wake you?"

"Hell, no," he said. "The guy called, and I've been up since then, waiting to hear from you."

"Where does he want to meet you?"

"I don't know why," he said, "but McCarran Airport."

"That's an odd place to make a blackmail payment. He really wants to do this out in the open."

"I thought blackmailers operated in the shadows," Lewis said.

"Yeah, well, not this one," I said. "At least we'll get a good look at him."

"Not really," he said.

"Tell me."

"He wants me to put the money in a trash can."

"I thought you were supposed to meet with him."

"Looks like he changed his mind."

"What time does he want you to do this?"

"Nine fifteen, aye-em," he said. "Why nine-fifteen?"

"That's probably the arrival time for a flight from L.A.," I said.

"Oh," he said, "I guess that makes sense."

"I'll pick you up at eight a.m.," I told him.

"I'll be ready."

"Get some sleep."

"Yeah, right."

***

I called Sammy's room and got no answer. He wasn't in his room, and he wasn't on stage. That left only one other place, which meant I was going to have to go and listen to Jerry Vale, after all.

Oye.

***

I entered the lounge while Vale was in the middle of a song, saw Sammy sitting at a front table, with a drink, a cigarette and a smile. I walked over and sat across from

195

him. He saw me and raised his eyebrows. I pointed to the bar, then stood up and walked to the furthest end of it. He followed. We never would've been able to hear each other sitting that close to Jerry Vale.

"What's shakin', Dad?" he asked.

"I just talked to Jerry," I said. "We should be gettin' it done tomorrow."

"I'd ask 'gettin' what done?' but ya wouldn't tell me, wouldja?"

"I can't—"

"Yeah, yeah," Sam said, waving a hand. "Just let me know when it's all over, because maybe then he'll loosen up."

"Will do."

"Listen, I gotta go back to my seat. Jerry's gonna introduce me and maybe bring me up on stage for a song. Stick around."

"I can't," I said. "I've got to get home. I'm pickin' Jerry up early."

"Your loss," Sammy said.

We left the bar. He went to his seat, and I got out of there. I wondered if Vale was going to try to get Sammy to sing in Italian?

## Chapter Forty-Five

I decided to spend the night at the Sands. I knew if I went home to sleep, Hargrove would wake me up early, drag me out of bed and probably to his office to question me about Leo McKern. He knew I was aware of McKern, because he had given me the file. He was going to roust me, Danny and Jerry, if he found out the big guy was in Vegas.

I had to get up, collect Jerry Lewis and get out of there before Hargrove realized I wasn't home, because he'd definitely try the Sands next.

I kept a room and a limited wardrobe in the hotel for nights like this, so I got up, dressed and went to Lewis' room. As I approached the door it opened, and a girl stepped out, looking disheveled, as if she had dressed quickly. After she closed the door she turned, saw me and froze. I saw it was Lila, the cigarette girl who had told me that Jerry wasn't funny.

"Oh, hey, Eddie," she said, embarrassed. She slipped past me and hurried to the elevator.

\*\*\*

When Jerry answered the door, he was chewing for real. I saw a room service cart by the sofa.

"I saw Lila leavin'," I said.

"Yeah," he said, "she's a sweet kid."

I stared at him.

"What?" he said, as if detecting some disapproval. "You gonna tell me I got a wife and kids at home? What are you, a boy scout?"

"Like you said," I replied, "she's a nice kid."

"Yeah, well, don't worry," he said, with a wave, "it was a one-night thing. Look, there's toast," he said, waving at the cart. "Help yourself. I gotta change my socks."

"What's wrong with the ones you've got on?"

He turned and looked at me.

"I've had these on for an hour. I change my socks five or six times a day," he said. "It's just . . . a thing."

He went to the bedroom and I went to the cart and snagged a couple of pieces of toast, hit them with some jelly and wolfed them down. There was also an extra cup there, so I poured some coffee before Lewis came back out.

"You ready?" he asked.

He was wearing grey pants, a red sweater with a yellow shirt beneath it, and loafers with yellow socks.

"Not exactly sedate," I said.

"What the hell's the difference?" he asked. "We're going to be in a goddamned airport!"

Good point.

"Let's go, then."

\*\*\*

When we got to the sedan in the back parking lot he said, "You know, I thought you'd be driving a Caddy, or something."

"This is a loaner," I said. "The Caddy's in the shop."

And it was. I had called my mechanic and had him pick the Caddy up from Henderson. He almost cried, but said he knew a good body guy.

We had stopped at the cages first to collect the fifty grand. The head teller, Sam Bishop, gave me the fisheye as he counted out the money and stuffed it into a canvas bag for us. He was tighter with a buck than Jack Entratter was. You'd think it was his money.

I drove to McCarran Airport and parked, and we went through the front doors. I hung back just a bit, so it wouldn't be obvious that we were together. We stopped at the magazine stand, so it looked like we were both searching for something to read. I grabbed a magazine without really seeing it. Turned out to be a Playboy.

"You think the sonofabitch is here, watching?" Lewis asked, without looking at me.

"Probably."

I checked the arrival times and, sure enough, there was a flight getting in at nine-oh-five. By nine-fifteen the passengers should have been disembarking and collecting their luggage.

The trash basket the blackmailer had chosen was right in the luggage area.

"There it is," Lewis said, and started for it.

"Wait for nine-fifteen," I said, almost grabbing his arm. "Might as well not piss a blackmailer off."

He didn't respond, but stopped walking.

"Did you get somebody to watch this for us?" he asked.

"No," I said, into my Playboy magazine. "I didn't think you wanted anybody else knowin' about this."

"Well, you're right, but don't you have somebody you can trust?"

I had two people I could trust, but Danny and Jerry were busy elsewhere.

"I'm gonna hang back," I said, then. "You put the bag in the trash, and then walk out the front door. And saunter. Don't rush. If he's here we want him to see you leave."

"You don't think he saw us come in?"

"I hope not. Okay, go ahead. I'll stay here."

I turned the pages, then flipped the magazine so I could pull out the centerfold while he went to the trash can. He looked around—which I wished he hadn't done—and then stuffed the bag into the trash. Then he looked around again, looked at me—I *really* wished he hadn't done *that*—and headed for the front door.

When he was gone, I put the Playboy back and picked up a Life Magazine, so I'd have no distractions. Nobody headed straight for the trash can, except for a couple of kids, who tossed some remnants of ice cream cones in.

By nine-thirty no one had stuck their hands into the trash can to retrieve the money. Plenty of people had dropped trash in, though. That bag was going to be a pretty sticky mess. Whoever would be going through it would need rubber gloves.

I was hoping Jerry Lewis would remain patient and stay in the car, but suddenly I saw him at the front window, with his face pressed to the glass. It was almost like he was trying to be funny, but I knew different. I wanted to wave him away, but didn't want to attract attention. Thankfully, he backed off on his own.

By ten o'clock I had switched to Sports Illustrated, but now I was standing there too damn long. Anybody watching might wonder what the hell that guy was doing taking so long to pick a magazine? So I finally paid for a copy of Mad and carried it to a seat with me. I took a good look at Spy vs. Spy, but also kept my eyes on the trash can.

\*\*\*

By ten-thirty I was getting pretty impatient, so I could just imagine how Lewis was feeling out in the car. People were still dumping garbage on top of the money, and nobody had come anywhere near sticking their hands in there.

Suddenly, a guy appeared pushing a large rubber garbage pail on a cart with wheels. He stopped at the far end of the room and emptied a trash can into it. He continued that around the room, until he came up next to the can in question.

He didn't bother looking inside. He simply removed the top, picked up the can and emptied it into his big rubber one. Then he replaced the lid and shoved off. He never once peered into the can.

I got up and followed along as surreptitiously as I could. He continued emptying trash cans, and then started pushing his cart toward a set of swinging doors that said EMPLOYEES ONLY on them.

I walked over to the doors. They each had a window. I looked in, saw the man continuing on along a long corridor. Supposedly, he would be emptying his trash into a larger receptacle, like a dumpster.

Recently McCarran Airport had hired a new Chief-of-Security. His name was Harry DuPont, and he used to work security for several different casinos. He even did a six-month stint at the Sands, but didn't get along with Jack Entratter, at all. However, Harry and I had gotten along fine, though we never became fast friends.

I hadn't contacted him about this because Jerry Lewis wanted to keep it quiet. But I was sure I could get Harry to show me where the garbage was dumped without mentioning Jerry Lewis. That is, if and when I was stopped.

I stepped through the doors.

## Forty-Six

I made my way along the corridor. The garbage man had disappeared further down, and I was trying to figure out which door he'd gone through.

"Hey!" somebody yelled.

I turned, saw a man in some sort of jumpsuit approaching me. He obviously worked there.

"What are you doin' back here?" he asked. His jumpsuit fit badly, hanging on his bony frame, but I'd seen that plenty of times. Those things were rarely a perfect fit. He was also a little too young to project authority, but he tried. "This is for airport employees only."

"I know," I said, "I'm sorry, but there's another man back here who doesn't belong, and I have to stop him."

"Are you a cop?" he asked.

"No," I said, "I'm Eddie Gianelli, I work at the Sands. What's your name?"

"I'm Benny," he said. "I work in . . . baggage."

"Well, you can check me out with your security head, Harry DuPont. He'll vouch for me. But right now I need to find the guy who was collecting the trash. Do you know where he dumps it?"

"Uh, sure," he said. "I'll show ya."

He led the way along the corridor to another set of double doors, and through. Suddenly, we were standing in front of a group of dumpsters, and the smell of garbage was overpowering. There was no sign of the man I'd been following.

"Damn," I said, "where did he dump it?"

"Well," Benny said, "it has to be in one of these. You want to tell me what you're lookin' for?"

"I can't, really," I said. "I followed a man in here. He was short, kind of squat, in his fifties—"

"Sounds like Zack," Benny said. "He's worked here a long time, emptying garbage cans."

That meant he probably wasn't the blackmailer. But he collected the garbage and dumped it here, so the blackmailer was probably going to come to get it.

Unless he'd been waiting for Zack when he came in.

Which meant the money might be gone, and Zack might be in one of the dumpsters. But before I started looking, I wanted to try something else.

"Look," I said, "is there another way out of here?"

"Sure, in and out," he said. "Zack empties his trash, then wheels his cart out the other way."

I looked around.

"Where is it?"

"There's a door in that wall," he said. "You can't see it because of the dumpsters."

"Show me."

"Sure. Over here."

He headed over to the right wall and I saw what he meant. There was a doorway there, a single swinging door this time, rather than double, but wide enough for Zack to wheel his cart out.

"Where does it lead?"

"Into the baggage area, actually," he said. "The baggage from the planes is brought back there, and then we load it onto the belts."

I was in a quandary. Should I go looking for Zack, or search the dumpsters for either the money, or him? Or should I hide back there and continue to wait for the blackmailer? And what about Jerry Lewis? How crazy must he be going waiting outside?

"Look," he said, "I gotta go to work. But if I leave you back here, you could get in trouble, and I might get fired."

"I told you, you can check with Harry—"

"I know, but that'd take time."

"Look," I said, "just let me take a gander into these dumpsters, and then I'll go."

"Fine."

We walked back and stood in front of them.

"Which one would he have used?" I wondered.

"I don't know," he said, "left to right?"

That Old Dead Magic

"That's as good a reason as any."

I walked up to the first dumpster. They were all metal, the same size as the one behind the Carousel that Leo McKern had been found in. I lifted the lid to take a look inside, and then it felt like the lid came down on my head.

\*\*\*

The smell of garbage permeated my nostrils. I tried to wave it away, but that didn't do it. Then I reached out in the darkness, felt something above my head and pushed. The lid opened and light came in. I was inside the dumpster, lying on top of the garbage.

I rolled over, put my hand down to push myself up, but it landed in something slippery. I slumped back into the garbage and the lid slammed shut. I tried again, found some dry purchase, and pushed myself up. I was able to grab the side of the dumpster then, pushed the lid open with one hand, lifted my leg over and climbed out. Actually, I fell out, hit the floor pretty hard and laid there a minute. My head was hurting.

Then I blacked out, again.

# Chapter Forty-Seven

"Wakey-wakey," somebody was saying.

I opened my eyes when he slapped my cheeks again. I was looking up into a craggy face that was staring at me from beneath a battered fedora. Harry DuPont, Chief-of-Security for McCarran Airport, wore every second of his fifty-something years on that face.

"Harry?"

"Eddie," he said, looking incredibly sad, "what are you doin' here?"

"Help me sit up."

He gave me a hand and pulled me to a seated position on the floor. I leaned on my knees and fought some dizziness. Then I felt the back of my head. There was a lump.

"You all right?" he asked.

"I'll live."

I looked at my hand. At least there was no blood. He'd hit me with something designed to do the job, like a leather encased sap.

"You want an ambulance, Eddie?"

"No."

"You wanna stand up?"

"Not yet."

"Okay," Harry said, "so answer my first question. What the hell are you doin' here?"

"I was following a blackmailer."

"Ah," he said, giving me a knowing look, "is this about some Hollywood type?"

"Yeah," I said, "the drop was in one of your trash cans in the terminal."

"You saw the pick-up?"

"I saw—do you know somebody named Zack?"

"Oh yeah," Harry said, "he empties the cans. Is Zack involved?"

"I don't know," I said. "I don't think so. I think he just picked up garbage like always, and then brought the contents in here."

"Then what?"

"Well, either the blackmailer was waiting and took it off him or the guy waited for Zack to leave and then picked it up. Actually, Harry, I'm hoping Zack isn't in one of these dumpsters."

"From the smell of you, that's where you were."

"Yeah, I managed to climb out before I blacked out again. Somebody hit me—wait. Do you know a guy from baggage named Benny?"

"Benny?" He thought a moment, then shook his head. "No Benny, Eddie."

"Aw, fuck," I said. "That was the blackmailer."

"Or the pick-up guy."

"Yeah," I said, "either way, he hit me over the head and put me in the dumpster."

I nodded.

"Then he left with the money."

"Harry," I said. "You better take a look in these dumpsters."

"For the money?"

"For Zack."

"Aw, geez," he said, and stood up.

I stayed on the floor as he started opening lids and looking in. When he got to the fourth one, he took a look, then stopped.

"Eddie?" he said. "You better see this."

"Shit."

He came over and helped me to my feet and over to the dumpster. I looked inside and saw the body of a man.

"That's not Zack," he said.

"I know," I said, "that's the guy who said his name was Benny."

# Chapter Forty-Eight

Harry actually apologized when he said he had to call the cops.

"I don't suppose you can wait until I'm gone to do that?" I asked.

"I know you don't have a good relationship with the cops in this town, Eddie," he said, "but I'd be in real trouble if I let you go."

"How about if I promise to come right back?" I was hoping I'd have time to go outside and tell Jerry Lewis to head back to the Sands.

"Eddie . . . this fella's got his throat cut."

"I know," I said. "The question is, why don't I have my throat cut?"

"Are you disappointed?"

"Just confused."

"Is your Hollywood type outside?"

"Yes."

"Who is it?"

"I can't tell you that."

He pursed his lips.

"If I let you go outside to warn him, or get him, or send him packin', and you don't come back, I'll have to tell the cops about you," he said. "You'll be in even more trouble."

"I think the fact that you found me unconscious will keep me from bein' a suspect, Harry," I said. "I'll just go outside and be right back. Ten minutes. I swear."

"While you do that, I'm gonna call this in. You've gotta get right back here before they get here."

"I swear I'll be back, Harry," I said. "I wouldn't leave you hanging."

"If you do, you'll be hangin' yourself."

"Got it."

"Go!"

I ran through the terminal, with people staring after me because I was covered with garbage. When I got to the car Jerry Lewis was still there. He saw me coming and started to get out of the car, but I stopped him by grabbing the door.

"Holy—you stink. What the hell happened—"

"You have to get out of here," I said. "Take the car back to the Sands."

"What happened?"

"There's been a murder, and I can't leave. The cops are on the way."

"The police, Jesus, Eddie—"

"I'm gonna keep you out of it," I said. "I swear."

"Who did you kill? The blackmailer?"

"No," I said, "I didn't kill anyone. I got hit and tossed in a dumpster. When I woke up, the guy who hit me was dead."

"But is he the blackmailer?"

"I don't know!" I said. "Look, Jerry, you've got to go. I'll see you back at the Sands."

"If you don't get arrested."

"Take the car and go!"

I gave him the keys and he slid over into the driver's seat.

"Where's the money?" he yelled, as I started away from the car.

I turned, waved and yelled, "Go!" again.

He started the engine and drove off just as I heard the sirens. I ran inside so I could make a phone call before they got there.

***

I was standing with Harry DuPont in the terminal when the police arrived. Since Harry knew what he was doing, not only did some uniformed cops arrive, but the detectives came, as well. I was still lucking out, because it wasn't Hargrove, but his old partner, Detective Everett, and his new partner.

"Gianelli," he said. "I didn't know you'd be here."

"Ditto," I said.

"Harry DuPont," he said. "this is my partner, Detective Taggard."

Taggard's dead eyes studied me and Harry closely, since he'd apparently never met either of us before. He looked to have as many years in his pocket as Everett did. They were a good match.

"You stink," Taggard said to me.

"Oh, yeah," I agreed.

"So what's up?" Everett said. "Harry, you said somethin' about a body?"

"In a dumpster."

"Another one?"

"Another?" Harry asked.

"A couple of our guys got called down to Fremont Street about a body in a dumpster."

"Is that right?" Harry looked at me and I shrugged.

"Well," Everett said, "okay, why don't you show me yours and we'll start there."

"This way," Harry said.

# Chapter Forty-Nine

He led us through the double doors and into the back, where the dumpsters were.

"Which one?" Everett asked.

"The fourth one," Harry said, pointing.

Everett looked at the two uniformed guys and nodded. They walked to the dumpster, opened it and looked in.

"Oh yeah," one of them said. "There's a guy here. His throat's been cut."

"Okay," Everett said, "call for the M.E."

"Yes, sir," one of them said.

"You stay right there," Everett said to the other guy, who nodded.

"Okay Harry, what's goin' on?" Everett asked.

"Ask Eddie," Harry said.

"Why Eddie?"

"He was lying on the floor here, unconscious, when I found him."

Everett and Taggard both looked at me, their arms folded.

"So, you have a story to tell us?" Everett said.

"I do," I said, "sort of."

"Sort of?"

"Well," I said, "there's stuff I can tell you, and stuff I can't."

"This looks like a murder case, Eddie," Everett said. "There's nothin' you can't tell us."

"Then I'm afraid we have a problem," I said.

"No," Taggard said, "*you* have a problem. You know, Detective Hargrove says you're an asshole. And it takes one to know one."

"I like him," I said to Everett.

"We're gonna have to take you and Harry downtown, Eddie," Everett said.

"Not Harry," I said. "He didn't do anythin' but find me on the floor."

"What were you doin' on the floor?" Everett asked.

"I had just fallen out of a dumpster."

"What were you doin' in a dumpster?" Taggard asked.

"Somebody hit me on the head and dumped me in there."

"Who?"

"I'm not sure."

"The same guy who's in that dumpster?" Everett said.

"Well," I said, "all I'm sayin' is that I can't be a hundred per cent sure, but I'm thinkin' that the guy in that dumpster hit me on the head and put me in this dumpster."

Everett looked at Taggard, who walked over to my dumpster and lifted the lid.

"Looks like somebody was in there," he said, letting the lid fall.

"So he hit you and put you in this dumpster," Everett said, "and then you killed him and put him in that one?"

"I doubt that," Harry said.

"Why?"

"I told you, I found Eddie on the floor, unconscious."

"Okay," Taggard said, "so let's say it was the same guy that killed him. Or, this guy hit you, and then someone else killed him. Why not kill you?"

"That I don't know," I said.

"What do you know, Eddie?" Everett said. "Let's start with that?"

"I'm afraid not, gents."

We all turned toward that voice and saw a little man coming through the swinging doors.

"Kaminsky!" Everett said.

"Hello, Detective Everett," Kaminsky said. "Were you questioning my client without his counsel present?"

"He's not under arrest," Everett said. "Right now, we're just trying to clarify what happened at the scene. And your boy was here when we got here."

"He was here when I got here, too," Harry said. "Do I need a lawyer?"

"Why don't you just stand by as a representative of the airport," Everett suggested.

"I can do that."

"And you," the detective said to me, "why do you need a lawyer?"

"I called him before you got here," I confessed.

"Why?"

"I didn't want to take a chance, in case it was Hargrove who caught the case."

"I'm afraid," Taggard said, "that given Mr. Gianelli's past dealings with Detective Hargrove, that makes sense to me, Everett."

"Okay," Everett said to Kaminsky, "what do you need?"

"Some time with my client."

"You don't just want to be present while we question him?" Everett asked.

"First," Kaminsky said, "I have to ascertain if I'm even going to let you question him."

Everett blew out a breath of exasperation and said, "Go ahead."

## Chapter Fifty

Kaminsky and I stepped out into the rear baggage area, through the single swinging door.

"What gives, Eddie?" he asked. "You asked me to get right down here, and I'm here."

"I was here makin' a blackmail drop," I said. "I followed the guy who picked it up through these doors, to the airport trash dumpsters. I ended up in one dumpster, knocked out, and he ended up in the other one, dead."

"Is that it in a nutshell?"

"Yes."

"And do you want to tell me who was bein' blackmailed, and what with?"

"Uh, no." I said, "not unless I absolutely have to."

"Well, if and when we get to that point," he said, "you'll be covered by attorney/client privilege."

"But what about what I have to tell the police?" I asked. "Do I have to say who's bein' blackmailed?"

"Well, if it's germaine to the murder case, you can probably be forced to in court—"

"What if we don't get that far?"

"Why don't we do this?" Kaminsky suggested. "You tell them what you want to tell them, or what you can, and then we'll see where it goes from there."

"Okay," I said, "okay, let's see what happens."

\*\*\*

By the time we rejoined the others by the dumpsters, the M.E. had arrived.

"He's only been dead a short time," he was saying as we entered. "Less than two hours."

"We know that, Doc," Everett said.

"Then you don't need me anymore," the doctor said. "You can remove the body."

"As soon as a boss shows up and gives us the word," Everett said. "Thanks."

The M.E. looked like a kindly old country doctor, but he didn't have a bedside manner to match.

"You didn't even need me here," he complained.

"It's procedure, Doctor," Everett said.

"Yeah, yeah," he said. "I'll leave my techs here. As soon as you have the word, they'll remove the body."

"That's fine," Everett said. "Thank you."

Once the M.E. left, Everett turned to me and Kaminsky again.

"Are we ready to talk?" he asked.

"My client will answer your questions as completely as he can," Kaminsky said.

"Well," Everett said, "we'll see. Eddie . . . what the hell were you doin' here? Just tell me, don't make me ask questions that you're not gonna answer."

"Okay, Det—"

"And be damn glad I'm here and not Hargrove," he added, cutting me off.

"Believe me, I am," I said. "Look, I was here to make a blackmail drop. The money went into a trash can in the baggage claim department. Then I waited to see who'd pick it up."

"That wasn't smart," Taggard said.

"Let's let him finish," Everett suggested.

"Sure, go ahead," Taggard said.

"The money wasn't picked up. Instead, one of the maintenance staff was emptying the cans, dumped it into his cart and brought it back here. I followed, but I was challenged by another employee, who said his name was Benny. He said the fella who picked up the garbage was Zack. I got him to bring me back here, and I started to worry that the blackmailer might have been waitin' for Zack, and that he might be in one of these dumpsters. I was hoping against hope that the money bag would be in a dumpster and not him. So I lifted the lid and looked . . . and that was it. Next thing I knew, I woke up in the dumpster."

"That's obvious," Taggard said, then raised his hands in surrender before his partner scolded him, again, for interrupting me.

"I climbed out of the dumpster, fell to the floor and blacked out again. I woke up with Harry lookin' down at me."

"Anything else?" Everett asked.

"Yes," I said, "Harry told me there was a Zack workin' in the airport, but no Benny. That made me think that the man who told me he was Benny was actually the blackmailer, and that he hit me and put me in the dumpster. But when we looked in the dumpsters to see if the money or Zack were in there, we found, instead, Benny. So now I'm confused."

"So am I," Everett said. "Why did the killer not kill you when he killed this Benny character? And where's the money."

"And where's Zack?" Taggard asked.

"Maybe," I said, "Zack took the money."

"So you're saying Zack is the blackmailer?"

"Can't be," Harry said.

We all looked at him.

"Zack has worked here longer than I have, and he's kind of a simpleton. He'd never be able to pull off a blackmail scheme."

"So there's somebody else involved, entirely," I said.

I hadn't noticed that one of the uniformed cops was gone, until he came back in. The other one was still standing by the dumpster with the body in it, along with two morgue attendants. He went over to Everett and said something to him in a low tone. It surprised Everett, who then looked at me.

"Officer Nelson did a quick canvas of the terminal, talking to the employees."

"Did he find Zack?"

"No," Everett said, "but a couple of employees said they saw Jerry Lewis in the terminal."

"Jerry Lewis?" Kaminsky said. "I love him."

We all looked at him and he fell silent.

"Is Jerry Lewis at the Sands?" Everett asked.

"As a matter of fact, he is," I said.

"So is he the blackmail victim?" Everett asked. "I know you do a lot for the likes of Sinatra and Dean Martin, and other celebrities who come to the Sands."

"Sammy Davis is at the Sands right now, too," I said. "Why don't you ask me if he's the victim?"

"Is he?" Everett asked. "Is it one of them? And why?"

"I can't say," I answered.

"Do you really need to know that?" Kaminsky asked. "You're looking for a killer. What does it matter who was being blackmailed, or why?"

Everett looked at Kaminsky like he was an annoy-
ance.

"It speaks to the motive for murder, counselor," he
said. "We're looking for suspects, and if Eddie doesn't
want to be one, he better give us another one." He looked
at me. "Who's being blackmailed?"

# Chapter Fifty-One

"That's privileged information," Kaminsky said.

"What are you talking about?" Everett said. "There's no privilege here."

"The blackmail victim is a client of mine," Kaminsky said, "as is Eddie."

"So?"

"So for Eddie to answer that question would violate—"

"Maybe," Taggard said, cutting him off, "if Eddie was an investigator workin' for you, you could claim privilege, but—"

"He is."

"What?"

"My regular investigator is busy, so I needed to hire somebody else," Kaminsky said. "That was Eddie."

Everett gave Taggard a long look, because the man had pretty much supplied Kaminsky with that tactic.

"Look," Everett said, "I could just take you both in, then send somebody to the Sands to haul in Jerry Lewis and Sammy Davis and any other celebrity who happens to be on the grounds—"

"Don't do that," I said. "It would be bad publicity not only for the Sands, but for the police and Las Vegas."

"Give me another option," Everett said.

"Am I really a suspect?" I asked.

He frowned.

"Probably not," he said. "You and DuPont sorta alibi each other . . ." he looked at Harry, ". . . but I do want to talk to this Zack." Back to me. "But I could make you a suspect."

"Let me talk to the blackmail victim," I said. "If he says it's okay, I'll tell you who it is, but I doubt you're gonna find out why. I don't even know that."

Everett thought the offer over.

"Get out of here before my boss shows up," he said, then, "because he'd make me take you in. He's as big an asshole as Hargrove is."

"Thanks, Everett."

"Get back to me fast, Eddie," he said.

"Come on, Eddie," Kaminsky said, grabbing my arm. "Before he changes his mind."

Together, we headed back to the terminal, and then outside. We were walking to Kaminsky's car—a Corvette—when another police car pulled up and a cop with bars and braids on his uniform got out.

"The boss," Kaminsky said. "We just made it."

"He's gonna chew Everett's ass," I said.

"Only until you tell him who's bein' blackmailed," Kaminsky said. "Can you tell me?"

"Privileged?"

"Of course."

"I can't."

"Eddie—"

"I promised!"

"I don't see your car around here," he said. "You need a ride?"

"Thanks."

We got in and he started the engine.

"Is it Jerry Lewis?" he asked.

"Kaminsky!"

"Well, he was here," he said. "I'm just askin'."

"I can't say."

"Fine!"

We left the airport and he got on I-15, which paralleled the strip.

"So," I said, "what's happening with the Leo McKern murder?"

"How'd you know about that?" he asked.

"I was there when they found him."

He looked at me, then back at the road.

"Did you tell Everett that?"

"No, but he mentioned this was the second body found in a dumpster."

"If he finds out you were at both locations—"

"Let's see how long we can keep that between us," I said.

"He's not gonna hear it from me," he said. "Privileged, remember?"

"Thanks for that, Kaminsky."

"Yeah, I bailed you out, there," he said. "You owe me."

"I sure do."

"So then tell me," he said, "who's bein' blackmailed?"

"You tell me," I said, "was McKern your client?"

He looked at me again.

"So it's gonna be like that, is it?" he asked.

"Yeah," I said. "Tit-for-tat."

I didn't think he'd go for it, but he fooled me and put me on the spot.

"Okay, yes, he was a client."

"You knew Hargrove wanted him for those missing girls, right?"

"It doesn't matter," he said. "Everybody deserves a defense."

"I suppose you're right."

"So?"

"So what?"

"Who's the damn blackmail victim?"

I told him.

# Chapter Fifty-Two

As I got out of the car in front of the Sands Kaminsky said "Don't forget to tell Jerry Lewis he's my client. I love that guy!"

"I'll tell 'im," I said, leaning on the door. "I'll call you after I talk to him."

"Lemme ask you somethin'."

"What?"

"Do you think Jerry could've snuck in and hit you over the head? And then killed the blackmailer?"

I remembered that Sammy's original fear was that Jerry Lewis was going to kill somebody.

"I'm tryin' not to think that, Kaminsky. I'll talk to you later."

He nodded and roared off.

***

I went inside and intended to proceed directly to Jerry Lewis' room, but seeing people's noses turn up as I passed, I decided on a shower, first.

I went to my room to shower and change my clothes, then went to Jerry's room and knocked on the door.

"Jesus Christ!" he said, as he opened the door. "I've been going crazy waiting here."

"The cops had a lot of questions."

He was walking to the bar and stopped cold, turned and stared at me.

"Did you tell them about me?"

"No," I said, "but you were seen in the terminal. Probably thanks to that red sweater and yellow shirt."

"You're going to criticize the way I dress, now?"

For some reason I looked at his socks. They were green. He'd changed them, again.

"Never mind," I said. "I need a drink."

He continued on and got behind the bar, while I stood in front of it.

"Bourbon?" he asked.

"Definitely."

He made me one, but not himself. The ice clinked as he handed it to me, and as I drank.

"Tell me what happened?" he said.

I did. I told him everything from the moment he left the terminal. I even told him about seeing him with his face against the glass.

"Waiting was driving me nuts," he said. "I was trying to see what was going on."

"Well, it was all out of sight," I said.

"So . . . murder?" he asked.

"Yes."

"And the money?"

"Gone."

"So the blackmailer may have it," Lewis said. "The payment got made."

"Could be."

"Then we're done," he said.

"What?"

"That's all I wanted," he said, "to pay the guy off and get rid of him."

"Jerry, blackmailers don't usually stop with one payment," I told him.

"What?"

"He'll probably be back," I said. "That's why I was tryin' to get a look at him."

"So now what?"

"I'll tell you 'now what,'" I said. "The detective on the case wants to know who was bein' blackmailed, and why."

"Did you tell him?" he snapped.

"No," I said, "I told you I wouldn't."

"Good."

"But you have to tell him."

"What? Why?"

"Because a murder happened," I said. "And forget the fact that they might look at me for it, but you were seen in the terminal. You'll have to explain that."

"I'll just tell them I arrived—"

"You've been on stage at the Sands all week," I said. "You can't lie about it, Jerry."

"But . . . I don't want anybody to know."

"Look," I said, "all you have to do is tell him that you were bein' blackmailed. I don't think you have to tell him why."

"But—"

"I got you a lawyer."

"What? Who?"

"His name is Kaminsky. He's representing me in this, and to keep the information privileged, he's representing you, too."

"So if it's privileged information, we don't have to tell," he said.

"This is a murder investigation," I said. "They're not just gonna take no for an answer. They could get some sort of court order. Or arrest us."

"For what? We didn't do anything. I didn't do anything."

"You're right," I said. "I'm the one who was in the thick of it. They might arrest me."

He stared at me. I could see his brain going. If I got arrested, he'd be in the clear.

"Jerry," I said, "if they charge me with murder, I'm gonna tell them everythin'."

"You can't!" he said. "You promised."

"I may have promised," I said, "but I'm not gonna go to jail for you. Come on, you can't expect that of me."

He bit his lower lip and then said, "No, I suppose not."

"Let's just go to the police together—"

"Can we do this without me going to the police station?" he asked. "I—I don't want to be seen there."

"I could have the investigating detective come here," I said. "We could do it right here in your suite."

"That'd be better."

"I can call now—"

"Can we do it tomorrow?" he asked. "I want to think. I need time to think. And I have to go on stage tonight with Sammy."

"Are you still gonna do that?" I asked.

"Hey, Eddie," he said, "the show must go on, right?"

# Chapter Fifty-Three

I agreed to wait until morning before calling Detective Everett and asking him to come over. Now I had to check in with Jack Entratter and tell him the news . . .

***

"You what?"

"I convinced Jerry Lewis to talk to the police."

"You're involved in two murders?"

"Well . . . kinda."

"Kinda?" He sat back in his chair. "This doesn't sound like 'kinda', Eddie."

"Let's just say that two men I was lookin' for have managed to turn up . . . dead," I said, "but I had nothin' to do with either one."

"And your buddies?"

I knew he meant Danny and Big Jerry, both of whom he tolerated, at best.

"They didn't do it, either."

"Big Jerry didn't shoot somebody with that cannon of his?" he asked.

"Both men had their throats cut, Jack."

"That's not the work of a professional," he said. "That sounds personal."

"I know."

"Okay, and what about our waitress?"

"Gina," I said. "She's still missin'."

"And whose fault is that?"

"Take your pick," I said. "I gave Danny my okay to recruit her, he put her in harm's way, and Jerry was supposed to be lookin' out for us. We all fucked up."

"Or it's the fault of the asshole who took her."

"I like that a lot better."

"So what are you gonna do?"

"Tomorrow I'll bring Detective Everett up to Jerry's room and let them talk."

"Jerry Lewis is not a very forthcoming guy when it comes to his private life," Entratter said.

"He's not gonna tell them why he was bein' black-mailed," I said, "just that he was."

Entratter now sat forward in his chair.

"Once he admits he was bein' blackmailed," he said, "and that he was at the airport this mornin', that's gonna make him the number one suspect and take any suspicion off you."

"I don't think they really suspect me," I commented.

"Well, without Jerry you'd be all they had."

Something just occurred to me.

"Not necessarily."

"Well, who else is there?"

"Harry DuPont."

The name struck a bell with Entratter.

"Didn't he work here for a while?"

"Yes, in security," I said. "Now he's Chief-of-Security for McCarran Airport."

"I remember," Entratter said. "I never liked that guy."

We sat in silence for a few moments.

"Okay, so why would you say DuPont's involved?"

"He never said how he came to find me in that dumpster area," I said. "So stay with me here. What if he's the kidnapper? He hires Zack and Benny to pick up the money, then kills Benny and tries to pin it on me."

"And the money?"

"Zack," I said. "That's all I can figure. He gave the money to Zack."

"And he trusts him with fifty grand?"

"He said Zack was a simpleton," I answered. "He's probably just doin' what he's told."

"Are you gonna give this theory to Detective Everett?"

"Sure," I said. "Maybe it'll keep him from takin' me or Jerry in."

"By sendin' him after DuPont."

"I hate to do that to Harry if he's innocent," I said, "but how did he know I was there?"

"You ever ask him?"

"No," I said, "but maybe I should."

I stood up and headed for the door

"Where are you goin'?" he called.

"Back to the airport!"

## Chapter Fifty-Four

When I got back to McCarran, I went to the Airport Security offices. There was a young man on duty, and I asked to see Harry DuPont.

"Mr. DuPont isn't here," he said.

"Then where is he?"

"I don't know," the young man said, "He left after the police took the body away."

"And he didn't say where he was goin'?"

"No."

"Okay," I said, "I need you to find out somethin' for me."

"What?"

"The home address of an airport maintenance man named Zack."

"Zack who?"

"Hopefully," I said, "there's only one."

\*\*\*

Zack Dickson lived in a neighborhood in Boulder City that used to be inhabited by workers from Boulder Dam.

I drove there, pulled up in front of a once hastily assembled clapboard house. All the workers needed back then was a place to sleep, no luxuries.

I parked and went up the walk, stepped on the flimsy front porch and walked to the front door. When I knocked there was no answer, but I heard somebody moving inside. I knocked again.

"Come on, Zack," I shouted. "I can hear you in there."

More movement. It sounded like somebody was wrecking the place.

I stepped back and kicked the door open. As I walked in, Harry DuPont turned to face me. He was standing in the midst of carnage, holding a gun.

"What the hell, Harry?" I said.

"That simple—the money's around here somewhere!"

"So you're the blackmailer?" I asked. "Or did you just grab the money?"

"I had simple Zack take the money home with him, and now I can't find it."

"Well, where is he? Ask him where he put it?"

"I could do that," he said, "but I'd have to wait for him to wake up. I had to knock some sense into him."

"So you're tearin' apart his house to find out."

"That's right," he said, waving the gun, "and now you're gonna help me. It's gotta be here somewhere."

"Why would I help you find it?"

239

"Because if you don't, I'll plug you."

"You went through all that trouble to make me a suspect in Benny's murder, and you'd ruin it by shootin' me? Who do you think the cops will look at, then?"

Dupont's face fell, and he seemed to age ten years in the last ten seconds, putting him closer to seventy.

"Goddamnit!" he cursed.

"You better get out of here, Harry. I told the cops to meet me here."

"You're bluffin'."

"Try me."

He glanced around the room, as if one more look would tell him where the cash was.

"Okay," he said, then, "I'm not done, yet. I can get another fifty grand out of Lewis."

"Not when I tell the cops you're the blackmailer."

"They'd only have your word for that," he said.

"You should get out of Vegas, Harry."

"I will," he said, "as soon as I have my money."

"The cops are gonna look for you."

"I'll take my chances," he said. "Now step aside or I'll shoot you in the knee."

I stepped aside.

"Eddie," he said, when he was in the doorway, "stick to what you know at the Sands. Don't come after me."

"Hey, Harry?"

"Yeah?"

"You know a guy named Leo McKern."

"Never heard of him."

He turned and left.

I searched the house, found Zack lying on the floor in the bedroom. At first I thought he was dead, but then I remembered Harry saying he'd have to wait for Zack to wake up.

That was when he moaned.

## Chapter Fifty-Five

"He was my friend," Zack complained. "Why did he hurt me? And tear up my house?"

We were sitting in his living room, where I had righted the overturned sofa.

"He's not your friend, Zack," I said. "He was just using you to pick up the blackmail money."

"Blackmail?" He looked confused. I didn't know what Harry had told him to get him to agree to pick up the money, but I guessed he hadn't mentioned blackmail. Zack apparently wasn't going to be able to support my claim to the cops that Harry DuPont was the blackmailer.

"He was here for his money, Zack."

"Yeah, that's what he said."

"You must've hidden it pretty good," I said. "What I can't figure out is, why didn't you give it to him?"

"I told him," Zack said, "I don't have the money."

"What?"

"The bag he told me to take," Zack said, "I never took it."

"Why not?"

"It wasn't there," Zack said.

"In the trash can? I saw it put there, and I didn't see anybody take it out before you collected the trash."

"No, no, I picked it up," he said, "but somebody musta took it outta my can."

"So it was never in a dumpster?"

"That's what I'm sayin'," Zack replied. "That's what I was tellin' Harry, and then he started hittin' me. Why'd he do that?" He looked confused.

"Because he thinks you have his money."

"But I don't!"

"Well," I said, "maybe I can convince him of that when I see him again."

He fell quiet for a few moments, then asked, "You think I can go back to work tomorrow?"

"Oh yeah," I said, "he won't be there."

\*\*\*

Fifty Grand was gone.

Unless Zack was a lot smarter than he looked.

I was going to have to tell Jerry Lewis to be on the alert for another phone call.

When I got back to the Sands, I checked for messages. Nothing from Jerry Lewis, several from Detective Hargrove, who needed to talk to me. I ignored them.

I called Lewis' suite. There was no answer. Then I realized he was probably still on stage with Sammy. So I went to the Copa Room.

Robert J. Randisi

I stood in the back and watched Sammy and Jerry Lewis. As usual, Sammy was all talent, and Lewis was all manic energy. And the audience loved them. Me, all that energy made me antsy.

I remained where I was until I sensed the act winding down, and then I went backstage.

To tell you the truth, I half expected to find Sammy up on stage alone. It wouldn't have surprised me if Jerry Lewis caught the red eye out of Vegas and left me hanging.

But there he was, coming off stage with Sammy, heading for their dressing rooms.

"Eddie, my man!" Sammy said. His eyes were shining—the glass one because it always did, and the good one with excitement. "What'd you think?"

"Fabulous, as always, Sam," I said.

"Tomorrow's our last night," he said. "Frank's gonna be here."

"That'll be great," I said.

Jerry Lewis had gone right past me to his dressing room.

"How was Jerry tonight?" I asked.

"Tense," Sammy said, "manic, crazy. What's happenin' with you and him?"

"We're gettin' there," I said. "I've got to talk to him now."

"Good luck," Sammy said. "He don't like anybody in his dressing room."

"He'll have to put up with me," I said.

"I need a shower and a drink," Sammy said. "I'll see ya."

While Sammy went to his dressing room, I headed for Jerry Lewis'. I knocked and walked right in.

"What the hell—" Lewis started to yell, but then he saw it was me. "Come in and shut the door."

I entered and slammed the door. He turned away from his mirror and looked at me, his face shiny with perspiration.

"You got news?"

"I had an idea where the money might be, and who the blackmailer was," I said.

"And?"

"I found the blackmailer, but the money's missin'."

"Missing?"

"He doesn't have it."

His eyes went wide.

"Fifty grand is gone, and the blackmailer doesn't have it?"

"That's about the size of it. Which means he should be callin' you again."

"But we know who he is now?"

"We do."

"Well, don't keep me in suspense," he said. "Who the hell is he?"

"His name's Harry DuPont."

"DuPont," Lewis repeated. "I don't know him. Who is he?"

"Oddly enough, his business is security."

"How the hell did he ever get anything on my father?" Lewis asked.

"He once told me he worked in the Borscht Belt for a while," I said.

"Really?"

"He must've been up there when your dad was performing. He might've got pictures, hung onto them. As you got bigger and bigger, he thought about it."

"What about when me and Dino were so big?" I asked. "Why wouldn't he have tried then?"

"Maybe he was doin' okay back then," he said, "but then he came to Vegas and started a downhill slide. Now he runs security in a small airport. He must've thought it was time to cash in."

"And now he has."

"What pictures did he show you?"

"He sent me one photo," Lewis said, "that in itself isn't damning, but he included a note that said he's got worse."

"Hmm."

"You don't think he does?"

"Harry's been known to stretch the truth."

"You know him?"

"He actually worked here for a while," I said. "Before he became head of security at the airport."

"So he's the guy who found you on the floor?"

"Yeah," I said, "that's what made me suspicious. How did he find me? Turns out he's the one who hit me and put me in the dumpster."

"Why?"

"He killed his partner and wanted the fish-eye to fall on me."

"So where is this guy? And who took the money?"

I told him about going to Zack's house in Boulder City, about finding Harry there, and him pulling a gun on me.

"So he had another chance to kill you?"

"Yeah, but I convinced him that if he did, all the suspicion was gonna shift to him."

"So when you have me talk to the cops tomorrow, we can tell them about him?"

"We can, and they'll know who he is," I said, "but they'll have to believe us."

"You can't prove it's him?"

"Right now, it'll be my word against his," I said, "but he might not be around to argue it."

"You think he's going to leave Vegas?"

"No, but I don't think he'll go back to his job," I said. "He's gonna try to cash in and then leave town."

"So he's going to come back to me for fifty thousand more?"

"That's what I figure."

"Sonofabitch!" he swore. "I wish you had killed him."

"That was never an option," I said.

"Oh, I know, I know," he said. "What about this other guy, Zack? Can't he back your claim that DuPont's a blackmailer and killer?"

"Zack's a little simple-minded," I said, "or he's pullin' one over on everybody."

"When will you be calling the police?"

"In the mornin'," I said. "You might as well have your breakfast, and I'll bring them up after that."

"I'll do room service."

"I'll leave you alone now so you can come down from your show," I said. "I'll call you in the mornin' just to let you know when we're on the way up."

"Yeah, okay."

I started for the door, then turned back to him.

"I'm just coverin' all my bases, Jerry," I said, "but if you're thinkin' about not bein' here tomorrow—"

"You're thinking I might hang you out to dry?" he demanded.

"Like I said, I'm just coverin' all my bases."

"Don't worry," he said. "I'll be here. Just make sure you also bring my lawyer."

"We'll be here."

I left his dressing room.

# Chapter Fifty-Six

Once again, I spent the night at the Sands, and swapped out pieces of my limited wardrobe there in the morning. Same grey pants as yesterday, blue shirt and a sports jacket.

Taking my cue from Jerry Lewis, I had breakfast brought to my room very early, and while I sat there and ate it, I called Detective Everett.

"I was hoping you'd call," he said. "I didn't want to have to come looking for you."

"I told you I'd call," I said. "Can you meet me in the hotel lobby at ten o'clock?" It was eight-thirty a.m. as we spoke.

"I'll be there, Eddie," he said.

"Do me a favor," I said. "Don't tell Hargrove."

"Wouldn't think of it," Everett said. "I'm enjoying watching him lather up about you. He's managed to get himself involved in that other dumpster case, so he's been trying to find you."

"He will, eventually," I said. "I'm not hiding." Not really. I was just . . . bobbing and weaving.

I hung up and called Kaminsky.

"Ten a.m.?" he repeated. "I don't know. I might have to be in court—"

"You wanna meet Jerry Lewis?"

"How about I show up at nine-thirty, so he and I can confer," he offered.

"I'll meet you in the lobby at nine-thirty."

\*\*\*

Kaminsky walked into the Sands' lobby at nine-twenty-five, decked out in one of his best black suits, the kind he wore to court.

"You're lookin' snappy," I said. "Is that just for Jerry Lewis?"

"I had court this morning," he said, "but I managed to get it postponed until later."

"Okay, well, maybe we can get this over with quickly. Come on."

We took the elevator to Jerry Lewis' floor and knocked on his door. He answered wearing red and yellow again, but with green socks.

"Good-morning, Eddie," he said. "And I assume this is my lawyer?"

"Kaminsky," I said, "meet Jerry Lewis."

"Mr. Lewis," Kaminsky said, sticking out his hand, "this is a real pleasure. I've enjoyed your work for years."

"Well," Lewis said, shaking his hand, "let's hope I'm going to enjoy yours."

He turned and walked back to the sofa, where he'd been sitting when we knocked.

Kaminsky turned and looked at me.

"I'm not even gonna come in," I said to both of them. "I'll wait downstairs for Detective Everett."

Kaminsky stepped inside, and I closed the door on them.

\*\*\*

In the lobby I used the house phone, got the operator to give me an outside line to call Danny's office. I didn't expect him to be there, but I was hoping Penny could give me an update.

"They're still out looking for Gina, Eddie," she said.

"What about the cops?" I asked. "Have they questioned Danny and Jerry about Leo McKern?"

"Yes," she said, "they were both questioned by Detective Hargrove. And Eddie, he wants to talk to you."

"I'll avoid him as long as I can," I said. "Did he give them a hard time?"

"He tried, but you know Danny and Jerry," she said. "They handled it."

"Okay," I said, "I'm dealin' with another problem—"

"The Jerry Lewis thing?"

"That's right. How much did they tell you?"

"Just that you were helping him," she said. "Oh, and they said that you told them he wasn't funny. Is that true?"

"Very true."

"That's too bad."

"Tell the guys I called, and that the Lewis thing has turned ugly."

"How ugly?"

"I found a body in a dumpster at the airport."

"Jesus," she said, "why dumpsters?"

"They're good places to put garbage."

"Can the two deaths be related?" she asked.

"I don't see how," I said. "Leo McKern and Jerry Lewis had nothin' to do with each other."

"Well," she said, "I hope you guys are done finding bodies."

"So do I, Penny."

As I hung up, Detective Everett walked in the front door with his partner, and one other person.

Hargrove!

# Chapter Fifty-Seven

"I been lookin' for you, asshole!" Detective Hargrove snapped.

"So I hear," I said. "Would that be about your . . . suspension?"

Hargrove gave the other two detectives a quick look, then gave me a hard one.

"Detective Hargrove caught us going out the door," Everett said, unhappily. "I said he could question you once we finished our business."

"Only I'm comin' along," Hargrove added, "so you can't disappear after."

"But he's going to keep quiet," Everett reminded the other man.

Hargrove grumbled.

"Come on, then," I said. "Jerry Lewis is waiting."

We took the elevator up, and when I knocked on the door, it was Kaminsky who answered.

"Ah, Eddie," he said, "and three long arms of the law. Come in, gentlemen."

"How did you get here, Kaminsky?" Everett asked.

"I told you at the airport, Detective," Kaminsky said. "Mr. Lewis is my client."

Everett looked past Kaminsky at Jerry Lewis, seated on the sofa, and asked, "Is that right, Mr. Lewis? Is this man your attorney?"

"He is, indeed. Why don't you gents come in and sit down? Can we get you something?"

"The truth would be nice," Everett said.

He and his partner, Taggard, entered the room. Hargrove followed, and then me.

"Not you," Hargrove said, putting his hand on my chest. He didn't shove, he just held me there.

"Eddie can come in," Jerry Lewis called out. "In fact, I'd prefer it if he was here."

"Let him in, Hargrove," Everett said, "and remember, you're supposed to keep quiet."

Hargrove gave me a dirty look, then removed his hand from my chest. I stepped in and closed the door.

"Find a seat, Eddie," Everett said, "and don't talk unless I ask you a question."

"Got it."

I went and sat at the bar.

Kaminsky walked around and sat next to Jerry Lewis on the sofa.

Detective Everett pulled an armchair over and sat across from Jerry and Kaminsky. That left Detectives Taggard and Hargrove standing.

"Okay, Mr. Lewis," Everett said, "we were told by McCarran Airport employees that you were there yesterday morning, in the airport terminal."

"I was."

"What were you doing there?"

"Eddie and me," he said, "we were paying a blackmailer."

"How?"

"Dropping the money into a trash can in the baggage claim area."

"Then what?"

"Then I went outside and waited in the car."

"That's it?"

Lewis shrugged.

"That's it."

"You never went back inside the airport after that?"

"No."

"Why not?"

"Eddie told me not to."

"Mr. Lewis," Everett said, "do you know who was blackmailing you?"

"Yes, I do."

"How?"

"Eddie told me."

"And how did he know who it was?"

"He figured it out," Lewis said. "And then he talked to the blackmailer."

"When did he do that?"

"Yesterday."

Everett turned and looked across the room at me.

"When were you going to tell me that?"

"When it was my turn to talk," I said. "Is it?"

"In a minute." He turned back to Jerry Lewis. "Mr. Lewis, why were you being blackmailed?"

"I'd rather not answer that."

"What if I told you that you had to?"

Lewis shrugged.

"I guess I'd let you throw me in jail."

"You'd rather go to jail than say?"

"Oh, yes."

"You wouldn't get that many laughs there," Everett told him.

Jerry Lewis leaned forward, grabbed a glass of water from his breakfast tray, which was still on the coffee table, took a sip, then said, "I'm not getting all that many right here," letting the water spill from his mouth down his chin and onto his chest.

Kaminsky and Taggard both laughed.

# Chapter Fifty-Eight

"You're not takin' him in?" Hargrove complained, as we left Jerry Lewis' suite.

"For what?" Everett asked, "Getting blackmailed?"

"How about tryin' to kill a blackmailer?"

"Come on," Taggard said, "Jerry Lewis?"

"You're impressed with him?" Hargrove asked.

"Hell," Taggard said "I love the guy. That water thing? Hilarious."

"Why do you think he had a lawyer there?" Hargrove asked.

"The same reason everybody has a lawyer," Everett said. "To cover his ass."

I remained quiet as I got into the elevator with the three bickering detectives. I pressed a floor button while they continued to argue. When the doors opened, they all looked out.

"This ain't the first floor," Hargrove said.

"No," I said, "it isn't. I thought since you guys still want to talk to me, we might as well do it someplace comfortable."

I got out of the elevator and they followed me—all the way to Jack Entratter's office.

"Jack," I said, after his girl waved us in, "you know Detective Hargrove. And these are Detectives Everett and Taggard."

"Gentlemen," Entratter said. "Welcome."

"Why are we here?" Hargrove demanded.

"Because I like to be kept in the loop," Jack Entratter said.

Before meeting Kaminsky at nine-thirty, I had called Entratter and set this up.

"Take seats, gents," Entratter said. "We're waitin' for one more person."

"Who?" Everett asked.

"Me," Kaminsky said, entering the room.

"What are you doing here?" Everett asked.

"Just seeing to my client's interests."

"Jerry Lewis?" Taggard asked.

"No," Kaminsky said, "not that client, this client." He pointed at me.

I moved some chairs over in front of Entratter's desk and we sat. All except Kaminsky, who sat on a sofa against the wall, and Hargrove, who remained standing with his arms folded across his chest.

"Okay, Eddie," Detective Everett said, "you're supposed to know who the blackmailer is. Why don't you enlighten us?"

"Harry DuPont."

259

"Harry—that old rummy runnin' airport security, now?" Hargrove asked.

Everett gave Hargrove a look that made him back off with his hands raised.

"Still not my case," he said. "I get it."

Everett looked back at me.

"Okay, tell me about it, Eddie."

"I found out the home address of that Zack fella who picked up the garbage."

"Yeah, so did we, in Boulder City. We went out there, and nobody was home."

"Well, I went last night," I said, "and Harry DuPont was there, kickin' the crap out of Zack and demandin' his fifty thousand dollars."

"Why would Zack have his fifty thousand?"

"Because Harry didn't have it," I said. "He had Zack pick it up from that trash can and bring it to the back. Only Zack and the money disappeared."

"And Harry and his partner dumped you in the dumpster," Everett said.

"And then Harry killed—what was his name?—Benny, and put him in another dumpster?" Taggard said.

"Hopin' you'd blame me for the murder," I said. "Or, at least, you'd hold me and question me long enough for him to get his money and leave town."

"So you're saying DuPont told you this."

"Not exactly," I said. "I got it from Harry, and then Zack."

"Zack's alive?"

"Like I said, Harry was kickin' his ass. I came in, and Harry pulled a gun on me."

"So he had a second chance to kill you," Taggard said. "Why didn't he, this time?"

"I told him if he killed me, that you guys would suspect him of everythin'."

"So he left you and Zack alive. And his fifty grand?" Everett asked.

"He doesn't have it," I said, "but he figures he'll just ask Jerry Lewis for another fifty grand."

"Are you buyin' any of this crap?" Hargrove demanded.

Everett looked over his shoulder at him.

"Quite a lot of it, actually," he said. "It makes sense."

"What part of this bullshit makes sense to you?" Hargrove asked.

"The reasons why Eddie is still alive, for one," Everett said.

"And you're really buying that a rummy like Harry DuPont could pull all this off?"

"Why do you call him a rummy?" I asked. "When he worked here, he wasn't a drinker."

Hargrove ignored me.

"If you're done with your buddy Eddie, I'm takin' him in with me."

"What for?" Everett asked.

"Questioning in the death of Leo McKern."

"Are you serious?" I asked.

"You were there, weren't you?" Hargrove demanded. "With your buddies, Bardini and Epstein? For all I know, one of you or all three of you killed him."

"I didn't even know Leo McKern," I said. "And I only knew his name because it was in the file you gave me."

"What file?" Everett asked, standing up. "You gave Eddie an official file?"

Hargrove put his hand out, like a traffic cop.

"That's not important."

"Yes, it is," Everett said. "It's against regulations. You could get into a lot of trouble for that. Wait a minute." Everett snapped his fingers. "Did you give it to him when you told him you had been suspended?"

"Well, yeah," Hargrove admitted, "but I was just tryin' to set him up."

"I knew it!" I said. "You were never suspended."

"He may not have been," Everett said, "but he may still be."

"What?" I said.

"What?" Hargrove squawked.

"I like where all this is goin'," Entratter said, with a smile.

"Whoa," Taggart said, "you're in trouble, Hargrove."

"No," Hargrove said, "no, I'm not. I can explain."

"I tell you what," Everett said. "You go down to the lobby and wait for us. When we're done here, you can explain."

"What?" Hargrove said. "You can't give me orders? You're not my superior."

"Maybe not," Everett said, "but I can get a superior over here in a heartbeat, and we can discuss regulations."

"No, wait," Hargrove said. "Yeah, okay, I'll go down-stairs and wait."

"Good," Everett said.

Hargrove glared at me.

"This isn't over, Gianelli."

"Good bye, Hargrove," I said, waving.

He snarled and stormed out of the room.

"That was fun," Everett said.

## Chapter Fifty-Nine

Everett turned his attention back to me.

"If there's anything you haven't told me, tell me now," he said.

"There's nothin'," I said, "except, of course, why Jerry Lewis is bein' blackmailed."

"What?" Entratter snapped. "Jerry Lewis is bein' blackmailed?"

"He didn't tell you, either?" Everett asked.

"I had no idea," Entratter said. He looked at me. "For what?"

"That's just it," I said. "He didn't tell me what for. It didn't matter, though. I was gonna help him, anyway."

"What about this Zack fella?" Everett asked. "Where do you think he is now?"

"I don't know," I said, "except that he asked me if I thought he could go back to work today."

"So he's at McCarran, then?" Taggard asked.

"Maybe."

"We can go and find out," Taggard said, looking at his partner.

"Yeah," Everett said, "let's do that."

"Okay, but I have to warn you," I said, "he's not the sharpest tool in the box."

"I'll keep that in mind." Everett and Taggard were ready to leave. "Eddie, be somewhere I can find you. Don't make me chase you the way Hargrove is," Everett said.

"I don't have any reason to avoid you, Detective," I told him.

"Just make sure you keep it that way. Mr. Entratter," Everett said, nodding to Jack.

"Detective."

They left.

As I stood up, Jack Entratter said, "Siddown, Eddie!"

I sat down.

"Tell me what the hell is goin' on."

I told him about the Leo McKern thing, explained that Gina was still missing, then told him about Harry, Benny, Zack and the airport.

"So Jerry's fifty grand is gone?"

"Missing."

"And the blackmailer is Harry DuPont?"

"Yes."

"And what's Jerry bein' blackmailed for?"

"I don't know," I said, not mentioning Danny Lewis. "It doesn't matter, Jack."

"I guess not," Entratter said, although I could see he wasn't happy.

"And that's all of it," I said.

"And Hargrove wants to jack you up."

"He's always wanted that," I said. "This time it seems he was taking a real active role, lying to me about being suspended, tryin' to get me to put my nose someplace where he could chop it off."

"Sounds like you got Everett on your side."

"Only because he's an honest cop, and he can't stand Hargrove."

"That's good enough," Entratter said.

"Let's see how long he can keep him off my back," I said. "What are you gonna do now?"

"Keep at it," I said. "Try to find Gina, try to find DuPont, try to find Jerry's fifty grand before DuPont can ask for more."

"And that was our fifty grand, right?"

"Uh, well, yeah," I said, "but I expect Jerry to pay it back . . . don't you?"

"I never expect anybody to pay what they owe without pressure."

## Chapter Sixty

What was there left to do but sulk?

First, I felt part of the responsibility for whatever was happening to Gina, and next I had let Jerry Lewis' fifty thousand dollars—advanced to him by the Sands—go missing. And third, I'd let Harry DuPont get away. Now he'd just bide his time and come back at Jerry Lewis for another fifty. Hopefully, he'd do it while Lewis was still in Vegas.

I was sulking in the lounge, sitting at a back table with a beer, when Big Jerry walked in.

"Hey, Mr. G.," he said, sitting across from me.

"Beer?" I asked.

He shook his head.

"Coffee."

I signaled the bartender for two coffees, and he brought them over and removed my partially finished beer.

"What are you doin' here?" I asked. "I thought you were helpin' Danny?"

"Now that Gina's missin'," he said, "the dick says I'm too noticeable."

"Ah," I said, "before he wanted you noticed, now he doesn't. I get it."

"Not even that," he said. "Before he was usin' me to keep Gina safe and then to back him up. Now he says he's gotta go places by himself, and can't have me—what'd he say?—'loomin' over him." He sipped his coffee. "It's my fault, ya know."

"What is?"

"That the kid is missin'," he said.

"No, we all had a part in that, Jerry. You, me and Danny. She never should've been involved. If she's dead, I'm not gonna be able to live with it."

"Me, neither."

"And believe me, neither will Danny," I added.

"So whatayou doin' now?"

"Well, I'm two-for-two," I said. "I also screwed up my blackmail job. The money's gone, and the blackmailer is still out there."

"But he got his money?"

I shook my head.

"He says no."

"Maybe he's lyin'," Jerry offered. "Ya know, so he can ask again."

I stared at him.

"Well, he's gonna ask again," I said, "but I didn't think of that." But if DuPont was lying, why was he kicking the stuffing out of Zack? Unless Zack was lying, too, and DuPont wasn't asking him for the money. Maybe there was some other bone of contention between them.

"It's all about lies, Mr. G.," Jerry said. "Usually."

"Jerry," I said, "you wanna work with me on this while Danny's tryin' to find Gina?"

"Sure thing, Mr. G. Whataya got in mind?"

"I'll tell you in the car."

***

The only connection to the blackmail plot that was still in play was Zack. And that was only if he went back to work. I still wanted to figure out my next play, and I thought I could do it by using Jerry as my sounding board on the way.

"How's the Caddy?" he asked, as we pulled out of the parking lot with me driving the sedan.

"Still bein' worked on."

"I'll pay fer the repairs, ya know," he said. "I mean, I had the car when it was damaged."

"Let's see what happens," I said. "My mechanic loves that car almost as much as I do."

"So where we goin'?" he asked.

"The airport." I explained to him about Zack and DuPont. He knew it was Jerry Lewis being blackmailed, but I still had not mentioned anything about Danny Lewis to anybody.

"So when you mentioned lies, I thought about Zack again," I said. "If he's not as simple as he wants people to think, maybe he was right there with DuPont on the blackmail, and maybe they had a fallin' out I interrupted that wasn't even about the money."

"What could it have been about if not the money?" Jerry wondered.

"I don't know," I said. "But if Zack really went back to work, we can ask him."

\*\*\*

I parked in the airport parking lot and went in the front door, to the terminal.

"Where does this Zack work?" Jerry asked.

"Maintenance," I said. "He emptied the garbage cans."

Jerry walked over to one of them and looked in it.

"Don't look like it's been emptied."

"There are dumpsters in the back," I said. "That's where we found the body."

"So one blackmailer's dead, one's missing, and Zack could be another one?" he asked. "Sounds like a crew."

"Sounds like a crew that's fallin' apart," I said. "Let's hope we don't find another body."

## Chapter Sixty-One

I would've checked with security before going through an Employees Only door, but I doubted DuPont would be around, and the security office might be in a little bit of flux. So I led Jerry right to those double doors and we went on through.

According to the board, we were there between arrival times, so the back hall was empty. There were no baggage guys running around. Last time I got stopped by "Benny"—still didn't know what his real name was—but this time nobody was there to challenge us.

"The dumpsters are in here," I said.

There were still four of them, and they hadn't been moved. Chances were, though, that they had been emptied since I laid in one.

"Jerry, do me a favor," I said. "You look in those two, and I'll look in these."

"What are we lookin' for Mr. G.?" he asked. "The money?"

"Or a body," I said.

"With all this desert around here to bury bodies in," Jerry complained, "why would anybody put them in dumpsters?"

"I don't know," I said, "but it seems to be a growin' trend."

Sure enough, both dumpsters had been emptied since I was there last, but had started to get filled up again. Neither contained money, or a body.

"Jerry?"

"Nothin', Mr. G.," he said, letting the lid slam on his second one. "Your boy Zack must still be walkin' around."

"If he is," I said, "let's find 'im."

First, I took Jerry through the single door that led to the rear baggage area. There were still no arrivals, so there was only a couple of guys there, sitting and waiting.

"Anybody seen Zack?" I called out.

They turned and looked at me.

"The maintenance guy?"

They looked at each other, then back at me and shrugged.

"Thanks."

We went back through the room with the dumpsters to the hallway. We could've gone left, back to the terminal, or right to . . . I didn't know where. Maybe there was a maintenance bay.

"This way," I said, turning right.

We followed the hall, looked in a few more door-ways—more dumpsters, some luggage, and some equipment. Also, a large hanger with two planes in it.

"We better go back to the terminal," I said. "If he's not there, we might have to check with security."

"DuPont's people?" Jerry asked. "Won't they be loyal to him?"

"It's more likely they're not very fond of him," I said.

*** 

Once we had checked the terminal and not found Zack, we went to security. The same young man I spoke to last time was still there.

"Mr. DuPont's not here," he told me, as we entered.

"We know that," I said. "We're looking for a maintenance man named Zack."

"Simple Zack?" he asked. "He's around."

"We haven't seen him."

"He might be in one of the planes, cleaning up," the man said.

I hadn't thought of that.

"In the hangar?"

"Yes. They wheel the planes in there so they can be cleaned."

I looked at Jerry.

"Back to the hangar?" he asked.

I nodded. As we turned to leave, the young man asked, "Do you know when DuPont is coming back?"

"Right now, Harry's on the run from the police," I said, "so I don't think he'll be back for some time."

The young man stared at me for a few seconds, then smiled and whooped.

"All right! I gotta tell Ralph."

"Who's Ralph?"

"He's DuPont's assistant. And, hopefully, he'll be the new security chief."

"All right," I said, "tell him about DuPont, and tell him Eddie Gianelli from the Sands is pokin' around here, lookin' for Zack."

"I'll tell 'im."

"Oh, and one more thing," I said. "How does Ralph get along with DuPont?"

"He hates him as much as the rest of us do."

"That's good." I looked at Jerry. "Come on."

***

As we entered the terminal again, Zack was actually coming out of one of the smaller passenger planes, maybe a 12-seater. He was carrying what looked like a bag of garbage.

"Zack!" I called.

He was coming down the steps from the plane and his head jerked over our way. At first, I thought he was going to run, especially seeing Jerry with me. The big guy's size was very intimidating, even with the weight he'd lost recently due to diabetes.

But in the end, he didn't run. When he got to the tarmac he stood still and watched us.

"Remember me, Zack?" I asked.

"You helped me with Mr. DuPont, at my house," he said.

"That's right," I said. "Have you seen him since then?"

"No." I saw something in his eyes I hadn't seen at his house. It made me think again that he may not have been as simple as he pretended to be.

"Zack, what was the fight that you had with Harry about?" I asked.

"There wasn't a fight," he said. "He was just . . . beatin' me up."

"But why?"

"I don't know," Zack said. "I done everythin' Mr. DuPont told me to do."

"And you still don't know what happened to the money?"

"The policeman asked me that this mornin'," Zack said. "I don't know." His hand tightened on the plastic trash bag he was carrying, and Jerry saw it.

"What's in the bag, guy?" he asked.

Zack looked at Jerry.

"Who's he?" he asked.

"He's with me," I said. "Answer the question."

"Garbage," he said.

He was going to run. I could see it. And so could Jerry. That was why the big boy was a footstep ahead of me, and Zack. As the man with the big bag swung around to take off, he momentarily tripped on the bag he was carrying, and that was all Jerry needed. He was on him and grabbed him in a bear hug.

"Lemme go, ya big fucker!" Zack snarled.

Now when I looked in his face the "simple" pretense was gone from his eyes.

"Drop the bag, guy!" Jerry said.

When Zack didn't, Jerry squeezed harder and that did it. The bag hit the ground, fell over, and cash fell out.

"Zack, Zack, Zack," I said. "So who's the brains, you or Harry?"

"Who'd'ya think?" he demanded. "DuPont's an idiot!"

"So you planned the blackmail?"

"That's right," he said, "and it woulda worked if not for stupid Harry killin' Benny. That wasn't part of the deal."

"Well," I said, "you're gonna have a chance to tell your story to Detective Everett."

"Look," Zack said, "there's fifty grand in the bag. I'll split it with ya."

"And what about Harry?" I asked. "Isn't he gonna want his cut?"

"Fuck Harry!"

"Do you know where he is?"

He didn't answer.

I sighed.

"Hang onto him, Jerry," I said. "I'm gonna call Everett."

# Chapter Sixty-Two

Everett and Taggard came to the airport, collected Zack and the money to take back to the station.

"I want to come along," I said.

"Eddie, you're going to run into Hargrove there."

"I don't care," I said. "I deserve to be on the close of this. If Zack gives you Harry—"

"All right, all right," he said, then looked at Jerry. "Him, too?"

I nodded.

"Him, too."

"We better get movin'," Taggard said.

***

When we got to the station, they put Zack in an interrogation room. Jerry and I were able to stand at a window and watch while they questioned him.

We got lucky to get that far without Hargrove seeing us, but that wouldn't last. Jerry had attracted a lot of attention, and Hargrove was sure to hear.

Zack sat slumped in a chair, still wearing his airport jumpsuit. Across from him sat Everett, while Taggard stood off to one side, leaning against the wall. The fifty grand was piled on the table between them.

"Look at it, Zack," Everett said, "because it's going back."

Zack didn't answer.

"What was with the dumb act?" Everett asked.

Zack shrugged.

"Just a way to get people to underestimate me, talk around me."

"So you'd know if they had anything worth stealing?"

Zack laughed.

"I'm not a thief," he said. "You'd be surprised the stories people tell each other when they think nobody's listening. Husbands and wives, both talking about who they cheated with while in Vegas."

"And you'd blackmail them."

Zack must've been proud of himself, because he kept talking.

"Yeah, but it was penny ante—until DuPont got the security job. He talked a lot, never gave me a second look. When I heard him yappin' about Jerry Lewis' father in the borscht belt, I knew we had something."

"So you revealed yourself to DuPont, huh?" Everett said. "Told him how smart you really are?"

"Sort of."

"What do you mean, sort of?"

"I told him just enough to make him think the whole thing was his idea," Zack said. "He even recruited Benny."

"Eddie says you didn't want Benny killed."

"No, that wasn't my idea. Harry didn't even mention it to me. That's what we fought about at my house."

"Not about the money?"

"Well, yeah," Zack said, "I had to be sure he wasn't gonna kill me, too, before I gave him the money—or, his share."

"So is that what you were going to do today?" Everett asked. "Get the money, and split it with DuPont?"

"Yeah," he said, "before Gianelli and his big goon stopped me."

"Where were you going to meet DuPont?" Everett asked.

"Why would I tell you that?"

"Because he's the one who committed murder, right? He's the one we want."

"So if I give you Harry, you'll let me go?" Zack asked.

"Not likely," Everett said, "but I'll tell the D.A. you assisted us in catching the killer."

"And what would that get me?"

"I don't know," Everett said, "leniency?"

"I tell you what," Zack said. "If I tell you where to find him, I want you to make sure he knows I told you."

"We can do that," Everett said. "By the way, what's your real name?"

"Zack Syndergaard."

Everett looked at his partner, who left the room, probably to check on that name.

"Zack," Everett said, "where's Harry DuPont?"

I saw a new look come into Zack's eyes—a crafty look.

"I think before I answer that question, I better have a lawyer."

I knew Everett had been hoping he wouldn't say that.

\*\*\*

"Do you have to stop just because he asked for a lawyer?" I asked.

"Gideon vs Wainwright from nineteen-sixty-three says we do," Everett said. "And I'm not Hargrove, so I can't ignore that."

"Okay," I said, "but I have an idea."

\*\*\*

When Everett walked back into the interrogation room, he had a man with him.

"Zack, this is—" he started.

"Kaminsky!" the lawyer said, putting his hand out. "I'm your lawyer."

Zack stared at Kaminsky with a bemused look as they shook hands.

"Detective," Kaminsky said, "I need a few moments to confer with my client, alone."

"Of course, Counselor."

Everett stepped out of the room. Kaminsky put his head close to Zack's, so we couldn't hear what they were saying. He had to make it look good. I also noticed Kaminsky eyeing the cash on the table.

They talked for a few minutes and then Kaminsky rose, walked to the door and knocked.

"We're ready," he said, when Everett opened the door.

Kaminsky went back to the table to sit next to Zack, while Everett sat across from them.

"Okay, so where's Harry DuPont?" Everett asked.

"I've assured my client that his cooperation will be taken into consideration when he goes to court."

"Yeah, yeah," Everett said, "no problem. Zack?"

"Harry decided to go and hide in the last place you'd look."

283

"And where's that?"

"My house."

# Chapter Sixty-Three

There was no way Detective Everett was going to allow me and Jerry to accompany him when he went to pick up Harry DuPont.

"I advise you to get out of here before Hargrove shows up," he said.

"Okay, we'll go back to the Sands," I said, "but would you let us know if you get him?"

"I'll give you a call."

"And what about the fifty thousand?"

"That's going into evidence," he said. "You'll get it back when the case is closed."

"I guess that'll have to do."

"Tell Jerry Lewis he'll get his money back."

I didn't bother telling him the money had actually come from the Sands.

Jerry and I managed to get out of the building without running into Hargrove. I drove the sedan again, and we headed back to the Sands.

"What now?" he asked.

"I'm guessing," I said, "that you must be hungry."

"Kinda."

"How about lunch at the Golden Steer?" I asked.

"Sounds good."

I changed direction and we went to the Golden Steer, on Sahara.

Frank wasn't sitting at his table, so the maitre d' allowed me and Jerry to take it. We all knew if Frank showed up, he'd just join us. But there wasn't much chance of that. It was still early for dinner, and there were plenty of empty tables. We'd probably be in and out before any kind of dinner rush.

"So, looks like you got the blackmail thing taken care of," Jerry said, after we ordered.

"If the cops get DuPont," I pointed out. "We still need to see if Zack was tellin' the truth."

"I think he was."

"Why?"

"I've seen guys make deals before, for a lighter sentence," Jerry said. "He had the look of a guy who thinks the fix is in."

"I guess that'll depend on Harry's story when he's taken in," I said.

"Oh yeah," Jerry said, "they're gonna turn on each other, big time."

"You don't even know Harry," I said.

"Don't need to," Jerry said. "I know the type. Neither one of these guys is gonna wanna take the fall alone. Not for blackmail, and sure as shit not for murder."

"I guess you're right."

"So now all we gotta do is find Gina," Jerry said.

"And if we do," I said, "Danny still has his problem, right? Trying to find out what happened to those other three girls."

"He really had his hopes pinned on gettin' that fella McKern to turn on his partners. With him dead, he don't have much."

"Well," I said, "if he's lookin' for another girl to use as bait, he better not come to me."

The waiter came with our steaks, and we both let the conversation lapse while we cut into them. I'd ordered mine with steak fries, but although Jerry shouldn't have had any kind of potato with his diabetes, he at least stayed away from the fried kind and ordered baked.

When we were halfway through with the meal and slowing down Jerry said, "You know me, Mr. G., I don't think you can take much of the blame for what happened to Gina. That was all the dick and me."

"No matter how you look at it, Jerry," I reasoned, "Danny came to me for a girl, and ended up with Gina. I just hope that poor girl comes out of this in one piece."

But given what had already happened to Leo McKern, I doubted it.

## Chapter Sixty-Four

We left the Golden Steer and went right back to the Sands. There were messages for me from Sammy and Jerry Lewis. Sammy's just said, "call me," while Jerry Lewis's became increasingly more strident, from "call me" to "what the fuck?"

I called Sam first, from a house phone.

"Glad to hear from you," he said. "Jerry's about ready to piss himself."

"I know," I said. "I'm on my way up to see him."

"Good," Sammy said. "We've got our last performance tonight."

"I'll try to make sure he's firin' on all cylinders."

"Cool," he said, and hung up.

I called Jerry's room next, and when he answered I said, "I'm on my way up."

"About ti—" he started, but I hung up. I'd had about enough.

"You wanna meet Jerry Lewis?" I asked Big Jerry.

"I sure do!"

We took the elevator up.

When Jerry opened his door, his eyes widened when he saw Big Jerry.

"What made you think you had to bring muscle?" he asked, backing into the room.

I entered with Big Jerry behind me.

"Jerry Lewis," I said, "my buddy, Jerry Epstein."

"I'm pleased to meetcha, Mr. Lewis," Jerry said. "I'm a big fan."

"You sure are," Lewis said.

"Jerry's not only a fan," I said, "he just helped me close out your blackmail problem."

"Close it out?" Lewis asked. "You got the guy? And my money?"

"We got one of the guys," I said. "The cops are pickin' up the other one as we speak."

"And the money?"

"We have the Sands' money," I said.

"Yeah, yeah, right," Lewis said, "the Sands' money. You fellas want a drink?"

"No, thanks," I said.

Big Jerry shook his head, remained standing behind me. Jerry Lewis stood in front of the sofa in his grey pants, yellow shirt and mint green socks. No red sweater, this time.

"When will you hear that they actually got the second guy?" he asked.

"I should be getting' a call tonight," I said.

"Well, if you hear before our midnight show, let me know, will you? That'd be a lot off my mind and then I could go all out."

"Yeah, as soon as I get the call, I'll let you know," I promised.

"I know Sam will appreciate it," he said. "He's got to be tired of carrying me." He pointed at Big Jerry. "Have you seen the show?"

"No," Jerry said, "I ain't been around."

"I'll leave tickets for you," Jerry said. "Great seats. Come and see us."

"Thanks, I will," Big Jerry said.

"Eddie—"

"I'm gonna be a little busy," I said, cutting him off.

"I was just going to say," Lewis continued, "why don't you get out there where the cops can find you?"

"That's a good idea," I said. "I should let you get ready for your final performance."

I left him standing there and waved at the big guy to follow me out.

On the way to the elevator Jerry said, "I see what you mean about him not bein' funny."

## Chapter Sixty-Five

It was early evening when we got to the hotel lobby. It wasn't check-in, or check-out time, so there wasn't much foot traffic, other than guests going to and from the casino to the hotel, or from the pool to their rooms.

"Jerry," I said, "did you and Danny get to talk to the manager of the Carousel when you were there?"

"No, sir," he said. "The body was found in the dumpster, and the shit hit the fan."

"Do you have any idea what Danny is doin' right now?"

"All I know is he's lookin' for Gina," Jerry said. "I don't know how, or where."

"I've got an idea."

"Good," Jerry said, "what is it?"

"Let's go back to the Carousel," I said.

"Let's do it."

"Don't you want to know what I'm plannin'?"

"Whatever it is, it's better than sittin' around here," he said. "I'm with ya, Mr. G., whatever it is. And if it's bustin' somebody up, I'm your guy, because I'm ready."

On the way downtown I explained my plan . . .

\*\*\*

When we got to Fremont Street, I parked down the street from the Carousel. As we walked there, we passed the alley behind the club, where the dumpsters were.

"You wanna try the back?" Jerry asked.

"No," I said, "let's go in the front. We're not hidin' anythin'."

We went around to the front and entered that way. Evening was approaching, and business was picking up inside the Carousel. Most of the tables were occupied, and many of the slot machines, as well.

I looked around, spotted my cigarette girl, Gloria. At that moment she spotted us, too and came over with a smile.

"You came back," she said. "I thought you forgot about me."

"Not much chance of that, Gloria," I assured her.

"Well, can I get out of this place?" she asked. "Did you get me a job?"

"Not yet," I said. "I'm still tryin' to find that girl."

"Gina?"

"Yes." I frowned. "Did I tell you her name?"

"I heard it," she said.

"From who?"

"Preston. The manager, remember?" she asked.

"Right, I do remember. And that's who I want to talk to right now. Where is he?"

"In his office. He's been there ever since the body was discovered in the back. He doesn't come out."

"When did you hear him say Gina's name?"

"Last night," she said. "I was passing his office and he was on the phone."

"And what did he say, exactly?"

"I'm not sure," she said. "I think he said somethin' about Gina makin' the difference."

I looked at Jerry.

"I think I should squeeze him until his head pops like a pimple," he said.

"Wow," Gloria said, "can I watch?"

"You don't like Preston?" I asked.

"None of the girls do," she said. "He forces them to . . . service him."

"And if they don't?" I asked. "They lose their jobs?"

"No, nothin' like that," she said. "They just get the crummy shifts."

"And has he ever asked you to service him?"

"Me?" She laughed. "I'm a cigarette girl. Preston's preference runs to strippers."

"Have any of the girls who work here ever gone missin'?" I asked.

"Well, once in a while one won't show up for work," she said. "You know, this ain't the kinda place you give two weeks notice to. But you mean missin' like nabbed, or kidnapped, right?"

"Right."

She thought a moment, then shook her head and said, "Naw, not that I know of."

"Okay," I said, "how do I get back to Preston's office?"

"Well, it's that one," she said, pointing to the door in the back. "But Hector, over there, will stop you. He's the new security guy since the thing with the dumpster."

We looked over at Hector, who was standing next to the door with his hands clasped in front of him. He wore dark pants and a dark t-shit that showed off his muscles. He was almost, but not quite as big as Jerry. But if it came right down to it, I would've bet on Jerry's raw-boned strength against Hector's body builder physique.

"Okay, thanks, Gloria."

"You want me to take you back there?" she asked. "I think Hector's kinda sweet on me, since the boss won't let him mess with the strippers." She wrinkled her nose. "Ya know, his private stock."

"No, I think you've done enough," I said, thinking about Gina. "I don't want anythin' to happen to you."

"Aw, that's sweet . . . but you're still gonna get me a better job, right?"

"You got it," I said. "Next week you'll be workin' at the Flamingo."

"And you'll have me knockin' at your door, handsome," she promised.

# Chapter Sixty-Six

Jerry and I walked over to where Hector was standing. Jerry stayed behind me.

"You're Hector, right?" I asked.

"So?"

"Hector, we'd like to see Preston."

"Your tits ain't big enough," Hector said. "Get lost."

"That's pretty rude," Jerry said.

Hector looked at Jerry, which meant he was looking over my head. Suddenly, I felt the back of Jerry's hand on my arm and he eased me aside so he could step up to Hector. Now the musclehead had to look up to meet Jerry's eyes.

"We just needja to tell the guy we'd like to see 'im," Jerry said.

"And I said get lost," Hector repeated.

"Hector," I said, "my friend doesn't like bein' talked to like that. I want you to take a good look at him. Your business is lookin' scary, his is bein' scary. You look like you could crush somebody's bones, but he's done it. That's his business."

Hector looked at me, then back at Jerry. I could see the muscles in Jerry's shoulders bunching beneath his jacket. He wanted to squeeze somebody's head. Hector's would be as good as anyone's.

The only muscle working on Hector was the one jumping in his jaw.

Finally, Hector's eyes slid away from Jerry's and he said, "Wait right here."

Hector went through the door, with a last look at Jerry.

"We better be careful, Mr. G.," Jerry said. "We don't know what he's gonna come out with."

"Reinforcements?" I asked.

"Or a gun," Jerry said, reaching inside his jacket.

But when Hector came out, he was alone and empty handed.

"The boss says he'll see you. Follow me."

Hector led us down the hall to one of the doors that had been locked when I was last there. He knocked and opened it for us.

"Gents," Preston said, from behind his desk. As Hector started into the room he snapped, "Not you! Go back into the casino."

"You sure, boss?"

"I don't see where you'd be any help to me, Hector," Preston said.

"But, he—"

"Get out!"

"Good," Preston said, "incompetent people give me a headache. You must get that at the Sands, Eddie."

"You know who I am."

"Everybody in this town knows Eddie G.," he said. "I'm Preston Dalton, and I run this place." He looked at Jerry. "But I don't know this big fella here, who scared the shit out of Hector."

"Jerry Epstein," Jerry said. "From Brooklyn."

"Mr. Epstein," Preston said, "A pleasure. Now, what can I do for you gents?"

"You can tell us where a girl named Gina Reynolds is," I said.

"Gina." Preston frowned. "We don't have a girl by that name workin' here. You check Glitz and Glam?"

"She ain't a stripper!" Jerry snapped.

"Well," Preston said, "she doesn't work here."

"We didn't say she worked here," I said. "Your buddy, Leo McKern, brought her here to hide."

"Hide?" Preston asked. "Who was the poor girl hidin' from?"

"She wasn't hidin'," I said, "she was bein' hidden."

Preston's television anchorman face lit up with puzzlement.

"I'm afraid you've lost me, Eddie."

"Tell me, Preston," I said, "were you shocked to find Leo's body in the dumpster out back, or did you put him there?"

"Leo?"

"McKern," I said. "The dead man in the dumpster. You didn't ask me who he was the first time I mentioned his name. I assumed you knew him."

"The man in the dumpster," he said, "was a customer, nothing more. He'd been in here many times. And as far as I know, he also frequented Glitz and Glam, next door."

"Look," I said, "we managed to get into your locked rooms the last time we were here. And it sure looked to us like you had somebody held in there, probably tied or handcuffed to a chair."

Preston sat back.

"If you could prove that, you'd probably have some police here," he said. "I tell you what, if you're lookin' for a place to hide a woman, why don't you try next door?"

"Yeah," Jerry said, "why don't we?"

There were two possibilities. One, Preston had recommended we search the Glitz and Glam strip club just to get us out of the Carousel. Or two, he was completely innocent. He didn't kill Leo McKern, and he had nothing to do with grabbing or hiding Gina, or any other girl.

"Does your owner ever come here?" I asked.

"Rarely," Preston said.

"And you're the manager?"

"Kind of."

"What's that mean?"

"It means that as far as all the people who work here are concerned, I'm a manager," he said. "But I'm really not. Those locked rooms you mentioned, I can't get into them."

"We did," Jerry said.

"Yes, by kicking them in," Preston said. "If I did that, I'd get fired—or killed."

"Killed?" I said. "Isn't that a little . . . drastic?"

Preston held up a forefinger, indicating he wanted us to wait, then stood up, walked to the door, opened it, made sure no one was listening, then closed it and returned to his desk.

"Look," he said, "I've been aware for some time that something . . . wrong is going on here, and next door. But there's been little I could ever do about it."

"And now?"

"I don't think the girl you've been looking for was being held in one of those locked rooms," he said. "I think Leo McKern was, until they killed him and put him in the dumpster,"

"So you knew McKern."

"I knew who he was," Preston said, "and I had seen him around here before—back here, where customers don't belong. And I've seen him come in and out of those locked rooms."

"So you're sayin' that you're not involved in whatever is goin' on, but you know who is."

"I'm saying I may know who is," he corrected.

"And you're willin' to give us that name?"

"If you keep me out of it," he said.

"We're gonna need proof that you ain't involved," Jerry spoke up.

"Isn't it enough that I'm giving you the name?"

"You might be throwin' somebody under the bus to save yourself," I pointed out.

"Okay, look," he said. He opened his top drawer and took out a gun. Jerry quickly reached inside his coat and produced his .45.

"Hang on!" Preston said, putting his gun on the desk. It was a revolver, probably a .38. "I'm just pointing out that I couldn've pulled this out and started shooting at any time. I chose not to."

"Put yours away, Jerry."

He did, but before that he stepped forward and plucked Preston's gun off the desk.

"Why don't we just call that a show of good faith," Preston said.

301

## Chapter Sixty-Seven

We decided we still couldn't afford to leave Preston in his office while we went next door to Glitz and Glam.

"We want you to walk us over there," I said.

"Why?"

"So you can't call anybody the minute we leave," Jerry said.

"I haven't shown you enough good faith?" he asked.

"I'm sorry," I said, "but no."

"Let's go," Jerry said.

"If you give me away," Preston said, standing up, "you're going to get me killed."

"We'll do our best not to do that," I said. "If anybody asks, you're givin' us a tour."

"I hope this works."

As we went out the door, I was thinking, me, too.

\*\*\*

When we came through the door, Hector turned to look at us.

"Relax, big fella," Preston said. "I'm showing them around."

"Yes, sir."

We started across the casino floor. Gloria watched us go.

"Who does Hector work for, Preston?" I asked. "You or the real manager?"

"The real manager put him in place," he answered.

"You haven't told us his name, yet."

"It's not going to mean anything to you," Preston said, "but his name's George Wiltz."

"Never heard of him," I admitted.

"Me, neither," Jerry said.

"He came here from Europe last year," Preston said. "As soon as he arrived and took over here, I got the feeling he had something other than gambling on his mind."

"And your owner?" I asked.

"Like I said," Preston answered, "He stays away. I think he's afraid of George."

"And are you afraid of George?" I asked.

"Oh, yeah," he said.

We had reached the front doors. Before we went out, I asked him, "Then why are you doin' this?"

"After seeing what they did to Leo," he said, "I want out."

"So why are you still here?"

"I can't just leave," he said. "They'd kill me before I got out of town."

303

"They?"

"George and his people."

We were outside the Carousel and I stopped.

"Wait," I said. "Did George bring his people from Europe?"

"Oh yeah," Preston said, "Greeks, Arabs, even Serbs."

"No Italians?" I asked.

"I don't think so."

I looked at Jerry.

"So if Danny's right and these girls are bein' taken for a white slave ring, it's bein' done by Europeans."

"Why do they have to come to Vegas for their slaves?" Jerry asked.

Now I looked at Preston.

"I'm gonna make some calls, and if you're lyin' to me, you'll be sorry."

"I ain't lyin'," he said. "They're usin' Glitz and Glam."

"Who you gonna call, Mr. G.?" Jerry asked.

"Well, Danny, for one," I said, "and then somebody I haven't called in a while. I just hope he'll talk to me."

"Who's that?" Jerry asked.

"Mo Mo," I said.

## Chapter Sixty-Eight

We went back inside to Preston's office, and he let me sit at his desk to use the phone.

I called Danny's office first, got Penny and told her to find him and get him over to the Carousel as soon as possible. Then I hung up and called Chicago.

"Is he there?" I said, when the phone was answered. "It's Eddie G., from Vegas."

"Hold on," the voice said.

I saw Preston lean over to Jerry and ask in a low tone, "Who's he callin'?"

Jerry leaned over and told him.

Preston's eyebrows went up.

"I *thought* that was what he sa—" he started, but stopped when I waved my hand.

"Eddie G.," Mo Mo Giancana's deep voice said. "It's been a while. To what do I owe this pleasure?"

"I don't know how much of a pleasure it'll be, Mo Mo," I said. I explained to him why I was calling, and he listened, never saying a word until I was done.

"European's usin' Vegas as the base for a white slavery ring?" he said.

"That's about the size of it."

"And what do you want me to do about it, Eddie?"

"I wanna get rid of 'em, Mo Mo," I said. "I've got Jerry Epstein here with me, and Danny Bardini, but I don't think we can do it alone."

"And when do you plan to do this?"

"Today."

"You got them spotted?"

I hesitated, then said, "I think so."

"You think so," He fell silent for a few moments, and I let him think. I could imagine him sucking on a big cigar while he did. "No cops?"

"No cops," I said. "I'm not really dependin' on them much."

"Can't blame ya for that," he said. "Okay, tell me where you are."

"The Carousel Casino, on Fremont."

"And where are ya goin'?"

"Right next door. The Glitz and Glam strip club."

"Strip club," he grumbled. "They're usin' a strip club in our town?"

"That's what I figure."

"If you're wrong, Eddie—"

"If I'm wrong, Mo Mo, you'll never hear from me again."

"That might not be good enough, Eddie," Mo Mo said, "sit tight." He hung up.

"What'd he say?" Jerry asked.

"He's sendin' somebody."

"Eddie G.," Preston said, with respect, "I knew you were connected in this town, but I didn't know you were *that* connected."

"Mr. G. is the man in this town," Jerry told him.

"So how long is this going to take?" Preston asked.

"I don't know," I said, "they could be comin' from Chicago, or they could be comin' from down the street. You better tell Hector not to try to stop them."

"Right." Preston headed for the door.

"I'll go with 'im," Jerry said.

"Good idea. Make sure they let Danny in, too."

I sat back in my chair and worried. I knew that Mo Mo was facing some jail time, due to a trial coming up. I hated to call him at a time like that, but I couldn't figure what else to do. Where else could I get the help I needed? But if I turned out to be wrong, I bothered him for nothing.

Jerry came back in with Preston.

"Listen to what he just told me, Mr. G.," Jerry said.

I looked at Preston.

"There's a door that leads from here right into Glitz and Glam."

"Why didn't you tell us that before?" I asked.

"I still wasn't sure . . . but when I heard you call Sam Giancana, I figured I better come clean."

"Okay," I said, "since you're comin' clean, do you know for sure that it's this George guy who's snatchin' the girls?"

"No," he admitted, "but I do know he's runnin' some kind of racket out of the club."

"And out of here?"

"Not so much, except he's got an office here, and always keeps it locked. I think the door to Glitz and Glam is in there."

"We'll have to kick it in," I said, "again."

"I don't care," Preston said, "but you might have to take care of Hector, first."

"I can do that," Jerry said.

"We better watch him to be sure he doesn't make any calls," I said.

"I'll watch 'im," Jerry said, and left.

As Jerry closed the door, Preston asked, "Does he work for Giancana?"

Jerry did, on occasion, but I decided to let Preston think it was more than that.

"Oh yeah," I said, "when Mo Mo wants somebody's kneecaps broken, or a cement overcoat delivered, he sends Jerry."

"Yeah," Preston said, "he looks it."

Suddenly, Preston seemed overwhelmed. He was caught between George Wiltz and Mo Mo Giancana.

"You better sit behind your desk," I said. "I'm done, here."

I got up and he slid into his chair gratefully.

"You think this Wiltz guy can go up against Giancana?" I asked.

"I don't think so," he said, "but I'll bet he does."

"Well," I said, "I guess we're gonna find out.

"What if he's running a racket and it's not the white slavery thing?"

"Then he'll have to answer to Mo Mo, and I'll be back at square one."

# Chapter Sixty-Nine

When the office door opened, Danny Bardini came walking in.

"What the hell is goin' on?" he asked. "Jerry says you called Mo Mo."

"I did," I said. "He's sendin' some men. When they get here, I want to go next door."

"You wanna take Mo Mo's men to a titty bar?"

"I think Gina's bein' held there," I said. "And maybe some other girls. I think it's the base of the slavery operation, bein' run by a man named George Wiltz."

Danny looked shocked.

"Where did you get all this?"

"Some of it I'm guessin'," I said, "and some came from Preston. He works here. Preston, meet Danny Bardini."

"And you believe him?" Danny asked. Then, to Preston, "No offense."

"None taken. I understand your distrust, but as I told Eddie, I want out. I just can't do it on my own."

The door opened again, and this time Hector came flying in. He crashed into the desk and slumped to the floor. Jerry entered, followed by five men.

"These are Mr. Giancana's men," Jerry said. "I thought it would be better if we didn't have to worry about Hector."

"Which one of you is Eddie G.?" one man asked.

"I am."

He took a step forward, effectively separating himself from the other four.

"I'm Rocco," he said. He had slicked-back, black hair, a dark complexion and—like the other four—was very fit. They all seemed to be in their thirties. "Mr. Giancana said you're the boss."

"You heard him," Danny said. "You're the boss, Eddie. What's the next step?"

"Preston says there's a door from here to the strip club." I turned to Preston. "Take us there."

Rocco took out a gun, and then the other four did, as well. Jerry joined the party, and then Danny.

"You're not heeled?" Preston asked me.

"Not usually."

Jerry took the gun he had taken off Preston's desk out of his pocket and handed it to me.

"He is now."

It was a thirty-eight, like I had guessed, and heavy in my hand.

As we all crowded into the hallway and followed Preston I shouted, "No gun play unless it's unavoidable!"

311

\*\*\*

Preston took us down the hall to a locked door which Jerry opened with one kick.

"This is the room we thought she was bein' held in," Danny said.

"Preston says it wasn't Gina, it was McKern."

"Shit, that makes sense," Danny said. "Then they dragged him out back and tossed him in the dumpster." He looked at Preston. "They probably wanted the cops to figure you for it."

"Shit," Preston said, "I didn't think of that."

"Which door?" I asked Preston.

"I don't know."

Jerry tried one. It opened onto a closet. Then he tried another one, in the back wall, and it was locked.

"That's gotta be it," I said. "It looks like a shared wall."

"Well," Jerry said, "let's get it open."

"First let's try to do it quiet," Danny said.

"How do we do that?" Jerry asked.

"Find a key."

Jerry went to the desk in the room and began going through the drawers. But in the end, he found the key hanging by a chain on the desk lamp.

He took the key to the door, stuck it in the lock and turned it.

"It's open, Mr. G."

"Let's go," I said, reaching for the door, but Jerry's big hand stopped me.

"You don't go first," he said.

"He's right," Danny said.

"You neither, gumshoe," Jerry said.

"He's right," Rocco said. "We'll go first. That's why we're here."

Rocco stepped to the door, with the other men right behind him. They were all dressed in black pants and T-shirts and holding guns.

I was really hoping I was right.

Danny and I stepped back and watched them all go through the door, followed by Jerry, who dragged Preston along with him.

"Ready?" Danny asked me.

"I'm ready." I held up the gun Jerry had given me.

"Don't put your finger on the trigger until you're actually gonna shoot," Danny instructed.

"Right."

We went through the door.

# Chapter Seventy

We were in a storeroom.

Beyond the front door I could hear the thumping of the strip club music.

Rocco went to the door and opened it a crack, then turned.

"It's a hallway," he said. "Like next door."

"So to the left, at the end of the hall, will be the club," Preston said. "To the right at the end of the hall, a door to the alley in the back, with the dumpsters."

"And along the way more doors, some of them locked," I said. "We're gonna want to look behind those locked doors."

"We're not gonna be able to open 'em quietly," Rocco said.

"That's where I come in," Jerry said.

"Okay," Danny said, "we're gonna need a man watching the doors at each end of the hall."

"You and you," Rocco said, pointing to two of the men who had come with him. "The others with me. Let's check these doors."

We filed into the hall. Two of them took up position in the hall to watch the end doors, while the others moved quickly to the others.

"Locked," Rocco said.

"So's this one," one of the other men said.

The music wasn't loud, but the thumping was there.

"Jerry," Danny said.

"If he kicks it in it might be heard," I said.

"With that music?" Rocco asked.

"Let's play it safe," I suggested. "Jerry, you kick in one door, Rocco, you do the other one."

"Gotcha," Rocco said.

Jerry went and stood in front of one door, Rocco the other. Danny and I stood behind Jerry, Rocco's two men behind him. Preston stood off to one side.

"Ready?" I said. "Now!"

They each kicked out at the door. Jerry's popped open after one kick; Rocco kicked twice and his opened. Jerry went in, with Danny and me behind him. We were in an office, with a desk, a chair, filing cabinets, almost identical to Preston's office next door.

"Damn," I said.

"Eddie!"

It was Rocco. I stuck my head out the door, saw him standing in front of his open door.

"You better come and see."

Jerry, Danny and I left our room and headed down the hall. As we entered, Rocco and his crew stood aside. Preston moved to look in the door, but remained in the hall with Rocco's other two men, still watching the doors at each end.

It was an empty room with three chairs in the center. All three chairs were metal, had metal shackles on them. They were affixed to the floor and almost looked like three electric chairs.

"Somebody was held prisoner here," Rocco said. "No tellin' how long." He looked at me. "Nobody's here now, but looks like you're right, Eddie."

"Well," I said, looking at Danny, "now we need to talk to somebody."

"You need Tommy," Preston said.

"Who's Tommy?" Danny asked.

"He's got the same job as me," Preston said. "People think he's the manager."

"Do you think Tommy knows more about what's goin' on than you do?" I asked.

"I think he'd have to," Preston said.

"Then I think maybe you and Jerry should go get him," Danny said.

"Me?" Preston asked.

"You're the only one he's gonna recognize," I said. "Anyone else and he might sound some sort of alarm. Are there Hectors over here?"

"Well, because of the naked girls, yeah, usually two of them."

I looked at Jerry.

"All I can say is, try to do it quietly."

"Okay, Mr. G.," Jerry said. He looked at Preston. "Come on."

They walked to the end where the music was coming from, and through the door.

"This could go real bad," Danny said.

"We better be ready, then," Rocco said.

"I noticed there are no dressing rooms for the girls back here," I said.

"They're in another part of the building," Rocco said.

We all looked at him.

"Yeah, I been here before," he said, "out front."

The thumping of the music stopped, and I hoped that wasn't a bad omen. It started up again, though, and there was no shouting or shooting.

Then the door opened again, a man I didn't recognize came through, followed by Preston and Jerry.

# Chapter Seventy-One

The man saw the rest of us standing in the hall, then walked toward us. When he reached me and Danny he asked, "What the hell is goin' on? This big guy stuck a gun in my ribs and said I had to come back here."

"What's your name?" I asked.

"Tommy Zane."

"Well, Tommy," I said, "my name's Eddie Gianelli."

Zane looked surprised.

"Eddie G.? From the Sands?"

"That's right," I said. "This is Danny Bardini, he's a private detective."

"And these other guys?" Zane asked.

"Well, Jerry is the big guy with the gun, and these guys are here . . . in case we need them."

Zane looked around, then asked, "And why would you need them?"

"I hope we don't find out," I said. "Let's get out of the hall. In here."

He looked at the doorway I was pointing to.

"You opened that?"

"We did."

"Look," he said, "you gotta believe me, I've never been in there."

"Well, you're goin' in now," I said.

"Move," Jerry said, prodding him from behind.

"Press, what's goin' on?" Zane asked.

"Looks like we're gettin' out, Tommy," Preston said.

Jerry shoved Tommy into the room. He stopped short when he saw the chairs with the manacles on them. Danny and I went in and stood so he could see us, and we could see his face. His eyes looked glassy and he seemed mesmerized. He must've been in his early thirties, but at that moment he looked pale, and older. He ran one hand through his greasy brown hair.

"What the—" he started.

"Can it, Tommy," Danny said. "We ain't buyin' the innocent act."

"Whataya mean—"

"You can't be runnin' this club and not know what's goin' on," I said.

"Oh yeah?" he asked. "You work at the Sands. Do you know everythin' that goes on there?"

"Yeah, it just so happens, I do."

"Give it up, Tommy," Preston said. "Tell them what they want to know about the girls and let's get out of this."

"Shut up, Press," Zane said. "You're gonna get us killed."

"No," Jerry said, prodding the man's back with his .45, "you're gonna get yourself killed."

"You wouldn't," Zane said. "Eddie wouldn't let you."

"Listen to me," I said. "One of the missin' girls is a friend of mine."

"And mine," Danny said.

"And mine," Jerry said, prodding him again.

"But that's not the bad news," I said. "See, none of us have to kill you. Boys?"

Rocco and the others all came into the room.

"Close the door," I said.

Rocco closed it.

"Your bosses are runnin' a racket in Las Vegas," I said. "And they're doin' it without permission, and without payin' tribute."

"Tribute?"

"This is Rocco," I said, putting my hand on Rocco's shoulder. "He and his boys, here, they work for Sam Giancana."

Zane looked shocked.

"What? Giancana?"

"That's right."

Zane turned and looked at Preston.

"Eddie called Mr. Giancana from my office, and these men were here in ten minutes."

"Jesus." Zane looked at me. "I didn't know."

"I'll bet your boss, George, he knew," I said.

"Mr. Wiltz? Why would he deliberately go up against Sam Giancana?"

"Maybe because he's not from here, and he didn't know any better," I said. "What we need to know now, Tommy, is where are the girls? Where's the last one they took, Gina? A blonde?"

"Gina?"

"Don't make me ask questions twice, Tommy," I said. "We're wastin' time. If your muscle decided to come back here lookin' for you, there's gonna be a lot of blood."

Rocco and his boys all pointed their guns at Zane, who swallowed hard.

"I'll ask you one more time. Where are they keepin' the girls?"

"All right, look," Zane said. "There were three girls here. They took them away last night."

"I don't know who they were."

I looked at Danny.

"Could be three more girls," he said. "I wonder if they've even been reported missin'."

"Probably not," Zane said. "They try to target girls who won't be reported."

"But three were," Danny said. "That's how I got involved."

"It's the tip of the iceberg," Zane said. "They've got another shipment of girls ready to go. These three were the last ones." He looked at me. "Your Gina is in that group."

"Okay," I said, "now we only need to know where they're bein' kept."

I looked at Zane and he looked away.

"Now!" Jerry said, prodding him hard with his forty-five.

# Chapter Seventy-Two

"Right here," he said.

"Right where?"

"Downstairs there's a basement. It's soundproof. They keep 'em down there until it's time to ship 'em out."

"Ship them out from where?"

"L.A.," Zane said. "They pull a truck up behind here, load 'em up and drive 'em to the docks in L.A."

"A boat?" Danny asked.

"They can't put 'em on a plane," Zane said. "Too many of 'em. And they're chained."

"But they can put 'em on a boat?" Jerry asked.

"A trawler," Zane said, "in the hold."

"Jesus," I said. "How many? How many is one shipment?"

"Ten, sometimes a dozen."

"How many are down there now?" Danny asked.

"I don't know exactly," Zane said. "I never go down there. My job's up here."

"You don't help them grab the girls?" Danny asked.

"No."

"And you've never given them one of the girls who works here?" I asked.

"No."

I turned my gaze to Preston, who was standing off to one side, watching.

"Don't look at me," he said. "My business is next door. I don't know what goes on in here."

"Whataya wanna do?" Rocco asked. "Go downstairs?"

"I don't know," I said. "Tommy, where's George Wiltz?"

"He's never here," Zane said.

"Come on," Danny said, "he's gotta come here some time."

Zane bit his lip, then said, "Okay, look, he comes when they're loadin' the girls into the truck."

"And what do you do while that's happenin'?" I asked.

"I stay inside the club," Zane said, "and never look outside. Those are my orders."

"They do it while the club is open?" I asked.

"Oh yeah," Zane said. "Mr. Wiltz once told me while all eyes are on the front, they do their work in the back."

"With how many men?" Danny asked.

"I don't know," Zane said. "I told you, I never look."

"Guess."

He thought about it a moment.

"I've never seen more than half-a-dozen," he finally guessed.

"What kind of truck?" I asked.

"It's different every time. Sometimes a panel truck, sometimes a ten foot, or fourteen foot that they use for hauling. It depends on how many girls they've got."

"And you don't know how many are downstairs right now?" Danny said.

"No."

Danny looked at me.

"Should we go down and get them out?" I asked.

"No," Danny said, "they'll have guards. There's bound to be some shootin', and somebody's gonna get hurt."

"So what do you suggest?" I asked.

"I think we should wait until tonight and hit 'em when the girls are in the truck.

"What about cops?" Rocco asked.

"No cops until after we have the girls," Danny said. "After that you guys can leave it to Eddie, Jerry and me and we'll call the cops."

"And take all the credit for savin' 'em?" Rocco asked.

"Unless you wanna hang around until they get here," Danny said.

"Hell, no," Rocco said. "Mr. Giancana would kill us. I think you got yourself a plan, shamus."

Danny looked at me.

"Works for me," I said.

"Me, too," Jerry said.

"And what do we do with these guys?" Rocco asked.

I looked at Preston and Zane.

"I think I've got just the place," I said.

## Chapter Seventy-Three

We locked the two "managers" in a room over on the Carousel side, along with Hector. We tied and gagged them so they couldn't raise an alarm. Then we went out back to figure out how to set up to wait for the truck.

The only cover back there was the dumpsters, so Rocco and his men would take cover behind them. Danny, Jerry and I would cover the mouth of the alley.

According to Tommy Zane the truck came for the girls between midnight and three a.m. That, he said, was everything he knew. He had nothing more he could tell us.

After we locked Preston and Zane away, we gathered in Preston's office.

"We've got a few hours before getting into position," Danny said.

"I got a question," Rocco said.

"Go," I said.

"How much force can we use tonight?"

I looked at Danny for the answer. This was his ballpark—his and Jerry's.

"I say as much as needed," he said.

"Jerry?" I said.

"I agree."

"That means we're gonna leave you guys holdin' the bag," Rocco said, "with dead bodies on the ground when the cops show up."

"Well," I said, "hopefully they'll be more concerned with the girls we found than with the dead kidnappers."

"Okay," Rocco said, "just so you know."

"Don't worry about it," I said. "The three of us have dealt with the Las Vegas police before."

Rocco looked at his watch.

"So what do we do for four hours?" he asked.

"Anybody hungry?" Jerry asked.

\*\*\*

Two of Rocco's men went out to the diner at the Horseshoe and brought back bags of burgers and fries. We all sat around Preston's office and ate them. We washed them down with cans of soda he also brought with them.

"I wish I had some coffee," Danny said.

"We could go back to your office and get some," Jerry suggested. "It's right down the street."

"No," I said, "then we'd have to drink Penny's coffee."

"Hey," Danny said, "she does the best she can."

"I can send my men out again," Rocco offered.

"No," Danny said, "let's all stay where we are. In fact, why don't you send one of your men to the front of the alley—just in case."

"I get it," Rocco said, "in case the truck is early."

"Right," Danny said. "he can hightail it back here and let us know."

"Gotcha," Rocco said. "Cheech, you go first. Brother will come and spell you in two hours."

Rocco's men were called Cheech, Buddy, Joey, Frankie and one they called "Brother." These were all names you would have heard growing up around Italian families.

While Cheech went outside, we had nothing to talk about but what we were doing. What if Zane was lying? What if there were no girls in a basement under the strip club? What if there was no truck coming?

"Why would he lie about all that?" Rocco asked, as Cheech reentered, having been spelled by Brother.

"He might be more involved than he says," Danny suggested.

"What about the other guy, Preston?" Rocco asked.

"This is his office, his desk," I said. "I've been through it, and there's nothin' unusual."

"Besides," Jerry said, "I believe him. He doesn't know what's going on."

"But what about Zane?" Rocco asked.

329

"I think he came around and told us the truth," I said.

"So we're back to waitin' for a truck," Danny said.

"Yup." I said.

"What happened with your Jerry Lewis thing?" Danny asked, changing the subject. "The cops manage to pick up DuPont?"

"I haven't been back to the Sands all day," I said, "so I don't really know."

"You know Jerry Lewis?" Rocco asked.

"He does," Danny said.

"That guy is so funny," Joey said, from his corner of the room.

"Yes," I lied, "he is."

"Who else do ya know?" Frankie asked.

"He knows the whole Rat Pack," Jerry said. "Especially Mr. Sinatra and Dino." Jerry's usual respectful reference to Frank and Dean was "Mr. S." and "Dino."

"Frank and Dean?" Buddy exclaimed. "Wow. What're they like?"

I was about to answer when the door slammed open. In the seconds before we realized it was Brother, we all managed to point our guns.

"Truck," Brother said. "At the mouth of the alley—and it ain't collectin' garbage."

# Chapter Seventy-Four

"Move fast!" Danny shouted.

Rocco and his men ran for the door, got out and behind the dumpsters before the truck managed to pull into the alley. The only thing that gave them time was that the truck was backing in.

Danny, Jerry and I went out into the casino and headed for the front doors. We were taking a chance that Wiltz or someone working for him might be coming in that way, but if we believed that Preston and Zane weren't directly involved, then Wiltz wouldn't be looking for them. He and his people would go right down to the basement for the girls.

As we made our way across the floor, Gloria the cigarette girl spotted us. She moved between us and the door.

"Is everything all right?" she asked.

"Gloria," I said, taking her by the shoulders, "Go home."

"What? But I don't have that other job, yet. I still need—"

I pulled her to me and kissed her to shut her up. It surprised her into silence.

"You'll have your job," I promised. "Now go home."

I let her go and followed Jerry and Danny out the door. The only way she wouldn't have another job was if I didn't live through the night.

Once we hit the street, we ran around the corner to the mouth of the alley and looked in. The truck was just coming to a stop. We all took our guns out. I was not as comfortable with mine as Danny and Jerry were with theirs.

"Do we know where the basement door is?" Danny asked.

"Apparently," I said, "it's the last one in the hall, adjacent to the outer door."

"It shouldn't take them long, then," Danny said.

"If they go down right away," Jerry said.

Danny and I looked at him.

"They might want to go and look at the girls, first," Jerry said, with a shrug.

We all stared down the alley. One man had gotten out of the truck in order to guide it while the driver backed in. But now he was in and they were all just sitting.

"What are they waitin' for?" Jerry asked.

"Not what," Danny said. "Who?"

"Wiltz," I said.

"And if he's comin'," Danny said, "it's liable to be in a car . . ."

". . . that he might be pulling into the alley, as well," I finished.

"We need another place to hide, and fast," Danny said.

"Across the street," Jerry said, pointing. "There's another alley and a doorway."

We all sprinted across the street and just as we crowded into the darkened doorway, a car came down the street, slowed, and pulled into the alley. It didn't go all the way down, however, just stopped right there at the mouth, so it could easily back out. The driver and a passenger got out and walked to the truck.

"One of them's gotta be Wiltz," I said. "Let's go."

Danny and I couldn't move until Jerry removed his big bulk. Then we all ran across and stopped at the alley.

"We can't move until Rocco and his boys do," Danny whispered.

"And that won't be until the girls are in the truck," I pointed out.

"They're gettin' out," Jerry observed.

Three men got out of the truck and greeted the fourth and fifth man. Once that was done, they went to the back door, which we had remembered to unlock.

"Okay, they're in," I said. "Let's get closer."

"Hopefully they didn't leave a man in the truck on watch," Danny said.

"We've got to be close enough to help Rocco and his boys," I said.

"I think they can handle these guys," Jerry said.

"And if we move closer, we give them the advantage," Danny said.

"Let's take the chance," I said. "I'll go first. If there's a man in the truck on watch, he may get out to warn me off, rather than sound an alarm."

"Good thinkin'," Danny said. "Put your gun in your jacket pocket.

I put the revolver into the right pocket of my sports jacket and stepped into the alley. I walked calmly toward the truck. It was a ten-footer, the kind people used for moving. As I got closer, nobody got out. When I reached it, I could see no one was sitting in it. I turned and waved to Danny and Jerry to come ahead. They both stepped into the alley and hurried to join me in front of the truck.

The area was lit by light poles, so I was able to step out and look over at the dumpsters. Rocco and his men saw me. He stepped out and waved. I returned it, then stepped back in front of the truck.

"Okay," I said. "Our guys know we're here."

"So now we just wait," Danny said.

# Chapter Seventy-Five

"How are we gonna know if they figured out somethin's wrong?" Jerry asked. "Maybe Zane was supposed to meet them."

"You said you believed he was tellin' the truth when he said he wasn't involved," Danny reminded him.

"I said that about Preston," Jerry said. "Mr. G. said he believed Zane."

"Did I?"

"Yes, you did," Jerry said.

"Well, I did, then."

"Then where are they?" Jerry asked.

"We don't know how many girls they have," I said. "It may take a while—wait."

A man came out the door, then a girl, then another girl, and another and another . . . all chained together. They were dressed differently, some in shorts and t-shirts, others in dresses, but they all walked the same—with their heads down.

"There's Gina!" Jerry said.

"How can you tell?"

"Those yellow shorts, they're hers," he said.

"Anybody could be wearin' yellow shorts," I said.

"Those are her legs." Danny and I looked at him. "Believe me, I can tell."

Gina was chained to four girls in front of her, and three behind—supposedly the three who had recently been sitting in those metal chairs we found. The girls were shuffling with their heads down, a few were whimpering, but they seemed to have been drugged enough to make them pliable.

"Eight girls," Danny counted.

"How are they gonna get them into the truck?" I said. "And how will we know when they do?"

We couldn't see what they were doing once they all got behind the truck. The last person to come through the door was one of the men who had gotten out of the car. I assumed he was George Wiltz.

"Rocco can see 'em," Jerry said.

"He's right," Danny said. "When he moves, we move."

Every so often I could see someone's arm or leg behind the truck. The men were talking to each other and laughing. From what I could pick up, I got the impression the girls were being lifted into it.

"Let's get ready," I said.

Jerry moved to the other side of the truck and peered around. From there he could see the dumpsters.

336

Then we heard a sound and didn't have to wonder how we were going to know the girls were safely in the truck.

The back door of the truck sliding closed, with a bang.

"Okay, everybody just freeze!" I heard Rocco shout.

And apparently, nobody did. When the shooting started, I saw the man I figured was George Wiltz run through the back door of the club.

Danny saw him, too.

"I'll follow him, you go around the front in case he tries to get out!" he shouted at me.

Jerry was gone, probably to join the firefight. As Danny took off, I turned and ran out of the alley and around the block. When I got to the front I ran into the club, stopped just inside. I was almost expecting to see Wiltz coming toward me, but there was no one. Just the customers, waitresses and the naked girls up on the stages. Oh, and Gloria, the cigarette girl. She was wearing her street clothes.

"Eddie, wha—"

"Did you see him?" I asked. "Did he come this way?"

"Did who come this way?"

"George Wiltz!"

"The owner? Is he here? I've never seen him before."

"So a man didn't come running from the back?"

"No."

337

I stopped and listened. With the pounding music, I couldn't hear any shooting from the back.

Then I looked around.

"Where are the bouncers?" I asked. "Doesn't this place have bouncers?"

"Usually," she said, "but our customers are pretty good. They don't want to be banned."

"So no bouncers tonight?"

She looked around.

"They were here earlier."

"Okay," I said. "I'm goin' in the back. I told you to go home."

"I was about to."

"Then do it."

I hurried through the club to the door, keeping the gun out of sight. As I went through the door, I brought my gun out. The hallway was empty. No Wiltz, no Danny. But from there I could hear the shooting outside—which suddenly stopped.

I ran down the hall, looking in each open door as I did. When I got to the back door, I looked out. Jerry, Rocco and his men were standing over two fallen men and had the others on their knees.

"Anybody hurt?" I asked.

Rocco and Jerry looked over.

"A couple of my men took some lead, but they'll be okay," Rocco said.

"Where's the boss?" Jerry asked. "Where's Danny?"

"They both ran in here, but they're not in the club, and they're not in any of these rooms. Rocco, can he get to the girl's dressing rooms from here?"

"No."

My eyes met Jerry's.

"The basement," we said, at the same time.

"I'm comin' with ya!" Jerry yelled.

"Get Gina and the other girls out of the truck," I said. "I'll be okay."

I thought Gina would be calmed if she saw Jerry first thing.

I found the basement door, held the gun out, and went down the stairs.

## Chapter Seventy-Six

When I got to the basement, the first thing I saw was George Wiltz, gun in hand, sitting on the floor with his back to the wall, legs splayed out. Then I turned to look for Danny. He was in a similar position, against the opposite wall. There was only one difference.

Wiltz was dead.

Danny was alive, but bleeding from the right shoulder.

"He didn't leave me any choice," Danny said, as I crouched over him. "We fired at about the same time."

"I'll get you out of here, buddy."

"Check him first," Danny said. "Make sure he's dead, and check his pockets."

"For what?"

"I.D.," he said. "I want to make sure he's Wiltz."

I should've thought of that, but I was worried about Danny, and what Penny was going to do to me for letting him get shot.

I walked over to the man we hoped was Wiltz and bent over. First, I took the gun from his limp hand, then checked for a pulse. There was none. He was gone.

Next I checked his pockets, came up with a wallet that was stuffed with cash and i.d. The British driver's license confirmed that he was George Wiltz.

"It's him," I said, rushing back to Danny.

From the top of the steps I heard Rocco shouting down to us, "Hey guys, we gotta go."

I went to the stairs and looked up at him.

"Rocco, let your men go, but you get down here and help me with Danny. He's been shot."

"Right." He turned and shouted to his men to get lost, then ran down the stairs. Together we got Danny on his feet and helped him up the stairs.

"I assume that guy's dead?" Rocco said.

"Yes, and he's definitely the boss."

"Good," Rocco said. "Mr. Giancana will be real happy."

When we got to the top of the steps, we helped Danny outside. I saw all the girls were out of the truck, standing close to Jerry, who was holding his forty-five on the men who had been holding them. Gina was actually pressed up against the big guy, her eyes very wide.

And then we heard the sirens and saw two police cars pull to a stop at the mouth of the alley.

"Shit!" Rocco said, because he was trapped.

"Rocco, go!" I said, taking all of Danny's weight.

"Go where?" he asked.

"Into the club," I said. "Become a customer, and just wait there until the police leave."

"Good idea, Eddie," he said. "Thanks."

"Thank you, buddy," I said, "and your men. Tell Mo Mo I appreciate it."

"You got it."

He ducked inside the back door and ran down the hall to the club as the uniformed cops came down the alley, guns drawn.

"Everybody on the ground!" they shouted.

There was no choice but to obey. Jerry got to his knees and set his gun down on the ground.

The girls started to kneel, but the cops stopped them, recognizing victims when they saw them.

I helped Danny down to his knees, then knelt myself and set our guns on the ground. Two young cops came over and pointed their guns at us.

"What the hell's goin' on?" one of them asked.

"Call Detective Everett," I said, loudly. "He'll explain everythin'."

The two cops exchanged a look, then one turned and yelled, "Sarge!"

Thankfully, an experienced sergeant came over and took charge, putting a call in on his radio for a boss and the detectives.

By the time Everett came down the alley, there were ambulances on the street and a meat wagon. There was more dead than just George Wiltz, in the basement.

Danny was in one ambulance, the girls were in another two. Gina made sure she gave me a hug, and Danny a careful squeeze, before she went to the hospital.

"Thank you so much!" she sobbed, as did all the girls.

When Detective Everett arrived, he kept Jerry and me waiting, which we didn't mind. It gave us time to get our stories straight. He finally walked over to where we were leaning against the back wall of the building.

"So you guys did all this, huh?" he asked.

"Along with Danny Bardini," I said. "But when you give the story to the newspaper, you can say 'diligent detective work' solved the case of the missing girls. We'll back you."

"One of the guys you shot," Everett said, "claims there were five other men with guns shooting at them."

"Really?" I said. "It must just be that we were firing our guns so fast they kinda got confused."

"I had to reload twice," Jerry said.

"I'll take your guns for evidence," Everett said, and we handed them over. He had a uniform come over and stick them in evidence bags.

"You guys will have to come in and make statements," Everett said. "My partner's at the hospital taking Bardini's."

"No problem."

"And the guy in the basement?" Everett asked.

"The big boss," I said. "I think the white slavery ring's gonna be lookin' elsewhere for its girls for a while."

"You know," he said, "this was Hargrove's case."

"I know," I said, "that's why I told them to call you."

Everett couldn't help but smile.

"This is going to burn his butt."

# Chapter Seventy-Seven

We didn't get to the Sands until after noon the next day. Both our asses were dragging. We got Danny back to his place with his shoulder bandaged and his arm in a sling. Penny was there to fuss over him. Then we took Gina home to her place, where she was looking forward to a long, long shower and then taking to her bed, possibly for days.

In spite of the fact that one of the white slavers was claiming there were five other shooters, Everett finally filled out his report and only mentioned the three of us. None of us would see our names in the newspaper, which suited us just fine. Everett and his partner would get all the credit, and that would truly burn Hargrove's butt, as Everett had predicted. And he was probably going to blame me.

"Eddie G.! I been lookin' all over for you."

I turned and saw Jerry Lewis coming across the lobby floor toward me.

"Where've you been?"

"Busy, Jerry," I said. "Shooting some white slavers."

"Yeah, well," he said, "I've been waiting to hear if your cops got that bastard blackmailer."

"As a matter of fact," I said, "they did. Two of them. They're both behind bars." Everett had told me that just before Big Jerry and I left the police station.

"So I'm not going to hear from them again?"

"Not for a long time," I said.

"Eddie G.!' he exclaimed, happily. "I knew I could count on you. I'm heading for the airport now, so you have my thanks."

"One thing, Jerry," I said.

"What's that?"

"You *will* be hearin' from the police."

"What for?"

"You're gonna have to testify against these guys to get them put away."

"Jesus Christ, Eddie!" His happy face was gone. "I told you I wanted this kept quiet!"

"Well, murder kinda makes that hard," I said.

"If I have to go to court, will the judge make me tell them why I was being blackmailed?"

I didn't know if he would or wouldn't have to talk about his father in court, but I said, "Probably not. You better talk to Kaminsky about that."

"I have to use that little Jew as my lawyer?" he asked.

"I guess you can hire anybody you want."

"Good man." He slapped me on the shoulder. "I'll do that, the best lawyer in Hollywood. I'll see you guys."

He actually slapped Big Jerry on the shoulder in passing and headed for the door.

"What a shmuck," Jerry said.

"Yeah."

I went to the front desk for messages, found a ton from Jerry Lewis, a few from Sammy—who had already left town—and a couple from Detective Everett, who had told me he'd been trying to locate me to report about nabbing DuPont.

"So we found Gina, and you found the blackmailers," Jerry said. "What else is there to do?"

"Relax for a while," I said.

"I don't think so," he said, pointing. "That looks like somebody else who's been lookin' for you."

I looked where he was pointing and saw Grace Kaufman coming toward me with a determined look on her lovely face.

Well, there are ways to relax, and ways to relax.

"Grace," I said, as she reached us, "just the person I've been lookin' for . . ."

# Epilogue: *August, 2011*

Grace Kaufman turned out to be quite an experience in bed. Even all these years later, I wondered why I had been avoiding her? Of course, I didn't get a chance to relax until after she was done with me and had gone back home to her husband.

Despite my dislike for Jerry Lewis, I did feel bad for the way the telethon people cut him off. I have to admit to watching the telethon many times, especially the memorable one in 1976 when Frank Sinatra brought Dean out to surprise Jerry, and the two men embraced. Dean had sworn to me that it was Frank's idea all the way, and that Jerry was genuinely surprised. But I had to admit that I always felt there was a self-serving aspect to Jerry's time with the telethon. It kept him in the public eye when his career was at a low point. Could you really blame him for that?

Jerry did end up testifying in court, but his high-priced Hollywood lawyer earned his money and the name Danny Lewis never came up.

Gina got her job at the Riv. She told me later that she had picked up the book of matches at the Glitz & Glam while Danny was dangling her as bait on Fremont Street. It was one of the places he took her. Turns out she had them in her back pocket, so that even with her hand tied behind her back, she was able to get to them and shove them down the seat just before they took her out and put her in a van. One of the guys told the other that's where they were taking her.

I got Gloria the job I promised her at the Flamingo. Then she and I started seeing each other for a couple of months. The sex was good before she got caught stealing at her new job. After that she left town.

Detective Everett questioned the surviving white slavers, but never did find out where the girls were being sent. Apparently, only George Wiltz knew that. The girls we rescued told him whatever they knew, and then they all went home. Some of them had been reported missing, some hadn't been missing long enough for that to happen. Gina's mother called me and thanked me for saving her daughter. She said no matter what the newspaper reported, she knew it was me. I told her it was more than just me, but also told her she was welcome.

Hargrove bitched moaned and whined, and threatened me, Jerry and Danny. He also *actually* got suspended for a while.

Oh, and my Caddy? The vandalism had nothing to do with the case. Turned out it was just random.

I finished my bourbon and, since I was reminiscing, figured I deserved a little more, so I poured another finger—maybe a finger-and-a-half.

I thought briefly about possibly calling Jerry Lewis, checking to see how he was taking being dumped, but what would be the point? He never liked me, either. We saw each other a time or two over the years, were courteous, but never with any warmth between us. Sometimes I wondered if he was jealous of my friendship with Dean? But I knew there was nothing to be jealous of. Dean Martin and Jerry Lewis had a relationship that was special, and only they knew how unique it truly was.

So I put aside the newspaper and decided I had given Jerry Lewis enough of my time.

After all, how much time does a man in his eighties really have to waste?

# Coming Soon!

## Luck Be a Lady, Don't Die
## A Rat Pack Mystery
### Book 2

**Vegas, 1960. Gamblin', drinkin', and
everybody's misbehavin'.**

Six months ago, while they were filming *Ocean's 11*, the Rat
Pack needed Eddie Gianelli's help to track down the mug who
was sending threatening letters to Dino. Now they're back for
the premiere and it's Frank who needs Eddie's help. Seems a
babe he was planning to meet in Sin City took a powder—
leaving behind her luggage and a stiff in the bathtub. She's on
the lam, and it's up to Eddie to find her and figure out if she's a
victim or a killer.

**For more information
visit**: www.SpeakingVolumes.us

# On Sale Now!

## Everybody Kills Somebody Sometime
## A Rat Pack Mystery
### Book 1

"FRANK SINATRA and DEAN MARTIN never knew how much trouble they were in until Robert J. Randisi stepped onto the scene. A gem of a read!"

—SUE GRAFTON, author of *S Is for Silence*

**For more information
visit:** www.SpeakingVolumes.us

# On Sale Now!

## I Only Have Lies for You
## A Rat Pack Mystery
### Book 11

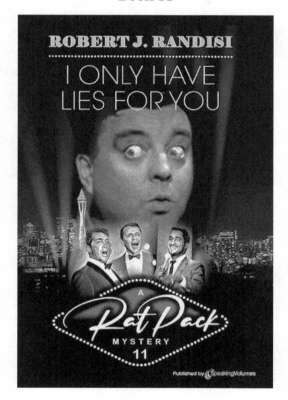

## For more information
### visit: www.SpeakingVolumes.us

Sign up for free and bargain books

Join the Speaking Volumes mailing list

Text

## ILOVEBOOKS

to 22828 to get started.

Message and data rates may apply.

CPSIA information can be obtained
at www.ICGtesting.com
Printed in the USA
LVHW011637070820
662641LV00001B/65